66 Laps

G·K
Hall
&C^{o.}

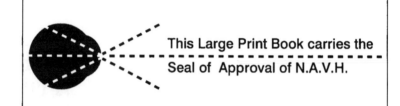

This Large Print Book carries the
Seal of Approval of N.A.V.H.

66 Laps

Leslie Lehr Spirson

G.K. Hall Co. • Thorndike, Maine

Published in 2000 by arrangement with Random House, Inc.

G.K. Hall Large Print Core Series.

The text of this Large Print edition is unabridged.
Other aspects of the book may vary from the original edition.

Set in 16 pt. Plantin.

Printed in the United States on permanent paper.

Library of Congress Cataloging-in-Publication Data

Spirson, Leslie Lehr.
    66 laps : a novel / Leslie Lehr Spirson.
      p. cm.
    ISBN 0-7838-9275-6 (lg. print : hc : alk. paper)
    1. Women swimmers — Fiction. 2. Married women — Fiction. 3. Adultery — Fiction. 4. Revenge — Fiction.
    5. Large type books. I. Title: Sixty-six laps. II. Title.
    PS3569.P5465 A12 2000b
    813'.54—dc21   00-061427

To my husband:
this will never happen

To my girls,
the reasons why

Acknowledgments

Infinite thanks to Joseph DeSalvo and Rosemary James of the Pirate's Alley Faulkner Society and my judge, author John Dufresne, for opening the door; to my agent, Deborah Grosvenor, for inviting me in; and to my editor, Bruce Tracy, his assistant, Oona Schmid, and Random House's Suzanne Wickham-Beaird for the warm welcome.

1.

I slapped the bitch. I didn't plan to, but that doesn't mean it was an accident. Some say life is one big accident, or a series of accidents, but that's not true. Accidents don't just happen. They happen when someone is careless. He didn't care any less; I cared too much about things that meant less. If only I could take it back, use my manners, let it go.

I carry the what-ifs with me, heavy as my heartbeat.

2.

The angry imprint of my hand swelled instantly on Colleen's cheek. Stunned, her eyes swept across my face like a spotlight searching for remorse. I was as scared as she was. But I wasn't sorry.

Little Gina started crying, her soft arms strangling my knees. Her tiny tears fought in vain to douse the heat of the moment. Colleen's son, already captive in his car seat, joined in. Without a word, Colleen bolted across the sun-baked driveway, climbed in her silver Jeep and squealed backward to the street. I pried Gina's grip loose, lifted her high and hugged her against my pounding chest. Her wail eased to a whimper.

Jim emerged from the corner of our yard where he'd been marking his territory. No stray coyotes would claim this stake. He zipped up his jeans, rounded the swing set and ran over. My husband is an extra-large kind of guy, rugged and boyish at thirty-eight, thick chestnut hair dipped in silver, with the kind of searing blue eyes that brand your heart . . .

8

until there is no more. Don't get me wrong, he's no pretty boy. He's a personal outlaw, a suburban cowboy, my hero.

"What was that all about?" He put out his arms for Gina.

I kissed her and handed her over to Daddy. I watched the Jeep barrel down the street and shrugged.

Frankly, I just didn't like the way Colleen said it. "Ooooh, you have gray hair!" — so gleeful, like it made her day. It made her day the last time she noticed, too. And the time before that. It was understandable that she had a problem dealing with the loss of pigment — after all, she lived off her looks. Maybe it justified the time and money she spent coloring her raven locks. Who knows?

At least she wasn't blond.

It wasn't that I minded my gray hairs. At thirty-two, I'd earned a few. Mostly, my chocolate tresses matched my eyes and flowed long and wild beneath the water, like a mermaid's. But in real life, each alien strand was a stop sign that shouted at me every time I looked in the mirror. Time's up! Over the hill! Move aside! Even so, I had no crisis when I turned thirty. I never lie about my age.

Jim waited for my explanation.

"She only made sixty grand modeling last year since staying home with the baby."

"Tough break."

I turned to see the smile I love so much. All summer in a smile. If I had long legs and big boobs, I'd be perfect for Jim. If he had a fat wallet, he'd be perfect for me. But someplace, a foot or so below the brain, we connected.

"Watch Gina, will you? I'm going for a swim."

3.

I slipped off my clothes and dove in the pool. We are 96 percent liquid. There is nothing more sensuous than a good splash against naked skin: the initial rush of cold, the smooth acquiescence of inner fluid to the outer mantle of wet.

I couldn't believe I hit Colleen. I was usually so polite, so full of shit. It's true, I never really liked her. She was an all-natural vegetarian: no sugar, no fast food, a superior being all the way around. Not that I could take the Twinkie defense, I was into being healthy, just not to a point of inconvenient excess. All things in moderation. Even moderation. Her son was the attraction. He was almost two, like Gina. Well, she had plenty of other friends who liked roly-poly bugs.

I eased onto my back, floating under a halo of fruit trees. Our yard was small, but perfect. The pool was heart-shaped; not like a perfect Hallmark heart, but like the real lopsided thumper that you live or die by. It was an oasis framed by a fading redwood fence. Drifting, I

11

could imagine valley living back when the condos were grapefruit orchards and the air smelled sweet and a person could see the pink mountains thirty miles away. Land ho! A horse neighed from a nearby ranch, a survivor. Gina loved our long walks around the neighborhood visiting the pig, the donkey and the old black-smith who still made house calls. We knew just where to find the old West among the decorative wagon wheels and dry wishing wells. We loved it here.

A shudder woke me from my reverie. A string of twinkling Christmas lights had slipped. It dangled down against the back of the house. Jim did things 100 percent or not at all. At night, our house sparkled from every angle. December was a memory, but the holiday spirit lingered. I used to think it was his sense of romance that kept those lights up all year long. Later, I realized it was laziness. I plugged them in one Memorial Day just to be a smart-ass. I fell in love with the instant magic — they looked so darned happy. After that we kept them plugged in. So it's romance after all.

Our pink crepe myrtle and a flowering white oleander framed a perfect palm tree in the distance. It was my own personal palm tree, rising up like a bottle rocket from a flare of fuchsia bougainvillea, exploding in a burst of languid fronds. My eyes slid slowly back down the long skinny trunk past the fence into the pool.

Time to get moving. I rolled over.

Thirty years of swimming has given me perfect form. Fingertips first, gliding under the surface, over the barrel, finish it off, elbows up. I breathed every other stroke, alternating sides on a good day.

I never felt finished unless I swam a mile. Sixty-six laps is a long way. Especially in a backyard pool designed for zebra floats and water wings. One circle equaled a twenty-five-meter lap. Sometimes it was just back and forth, back and forth, and I felt like I was trapped in a bathtub, counting down to freedom. Today, it was freedom. I could tune out everything, no one could get to me: no one could stop me. A hydraulic high. It didn't matter where I was going. Chances were good that I'd hit that perfect rhythm by lap 66.

Every life has a rhythm. The trick is to recognize the rhythm when you find it. Last September, I lay in the hammock with Gina, just after her nap. She was peaceful, sucking her bottle in the crook of my arm. I was lying there, loving her, loving Jim, loving life. The high trees were waving to me, telling me, this is *it!* The moment was joyful and content. The thrill of creation, the awe of immortality — the adrenaline rush of new motherhood.

But it was only a moment.

I tucked my head for a flip turn. My shoulders rolled forward, under. Nearly upside down, my hips twisted left by remote control. I

13

kicked out my feet to push off . . . but the wall was not there.

Panic. For the first time, I recognized the sensation of drowning. I lifted my head up, breaking the still surface of my peaceful world. I stood, stranded in three feet of water. What happened? I tried to catch my breath; instead, I caught my reflection.

A stranger stared back at me. The mutation was both subtle and violent. The invasion of gray hair at my temple, the triumph of blue veins trespassing on my thigh. I had slipped through the invisible hedge of adulthood. The voltage was high: the ravages shocking.

I was not old. But I would never be young again. I could no longer call myself a girl. I was a woman, and there was no turning back. I had reached my peak physically: now there was only downhill.

I had to find that rhythm again, that perfect rhythm, perfection.

I must have stood there for a few minutes, because Jim came outside with Gina naked in his arms. She squirmed to get down. They looked at me, two of a kind.

"Mommy!"

"You all right, darlin'?"

I laughed it off. I was fine.

"She wants to swim. How many more do you have?"

"I can't remember. I've lost count."

14

Fear swirled beneath my placid surface, like bile. I lost count once before, in a high school race. I relied on a boy squatting at the end of the pool with numbered cards. I was thinking about the race. He was thinking about my ass. I lost both.

I swore to maintain control this time. My dreams of youth were smothering. I wanted to swim farther, kick them into my wake and let them dissolve behind me.

Jim waited patiently for a more definitive response.

"I'm done."

He released our water baby and she ran right for the pool.

"Catch me, Mommy!"

4.

When I came out of the bathroom, Jim was hanging up the phone, laughing hysterically. I tucked a big green towel around me and scooped up my beautiful Gina.

"What's so funny?"

"That was the stage manager from the video I shot last week. Some babe wanted to know if I was 'really married' or just 'Hollywood married.' "

"Hollywood married?"

"You believe it?"

"What'd you tell him?"

"What do you think?" He pulled us into his lap and kissed me like he meant it. Gina rubbed her eyes. Jim noticed. He winked. "Nap time?"

"My hair's still wet."

"I love wet hair."

I smiled and put Gina in her crib. Who was I to dismiss romance provoked by outside interest? I was clearly the winner here. I wound up the mobile of teddy bears clinging to clouds that played "Over the Rainbow." Gina started

16

singing, made-up lyrics we'd lulled her to sleep with since she was born. Perfect sentimental accompaniment. I dashed into the bedroom and plunged into a jam-packed drawer of lingerie, searching for the perfect tool of seduction. Black lace, red lace, white lace, silk? Jim stepped behind me.

"You don't need that stuff."

Maybe not, but I liked it. Problem was, Jim was too tired — I take that back — I was too tired at night, and it was lucky when we caught a nap time when we were both in the mood . . . and the phone didn't ring . . . and Gina didn't wake up.

There was a time when I wanted him — no, needed him — to make love to me every day.

"I swear, we're a perfect fit."

"Mmmmm. Thank you, God."

Immersed in him, I lost myself. I lay on the bottom of the pool, looking up through the water at the airplanes flying overhead. They looked like UFO's from another world, another universe, another time. Water as a natural habitat. I was safe.

He rocked me to heaven. I clung to him, tasting my teardrops.

"Don't ever leave me."

"Shhh, never, never, never. I love you, Audrey. Shhh." He stroked my head, kissed my tears away.

Some women marry the answer to their dreams: I married the antidote to my nightmares.

17

The first time I saw him, I mean really saw him, I knew I had to have him. He had just gotten glasses and he looked so distinguished. I thought it was a temporary infatuation — after all, I was already promised. I kept asking my happily married boss, How do you know? How do you really know? My boss stared at his wife's picture on the desk. "You just know."

He was right. And the lucky part, not for my boyfriend, was that Jim knew I was the one for him, too. He was a bachelor stud, the one who always left with the beautiful babe at the end of the shoot. This I learned later — I only saw him as a kind, intelligent man. A real man in a noisy parade of boys. He wanted to make me happy and I wanted to let him. It seemed so easy. For some reason, which I still cannot explain, he burnt his little black book and accepted my proposal.

He didn't own a car or anything else much besides a mattress stained by years of grudge-fucking. We bought a new bed before he moved in.

He stopped having nightmares when I got pregnant. I never got the whole story and he never offered to tell. Not after that night in the kitchen when he got drunk and shoved me against the sink. He swore he'd never hit me and I left it at that. Better to bury the past than ✓ relive it, I guess, why spoil the mood? Ironic in a city where dogs have their own shrinks, but even my mother doesn't press. All I know is something happened that he didn't start but ended. Something bad enough to make a good kid leave home early and never look back. And who was I to pry? I got the benefit of his despair: all he wanted was a family, my family, me. In Jim's case, the future in my belly put a lock on his past.

But then, we all have our demons.

He started working with a passion and developed a passion for his work. No art school brat, he worked his way up from hey you to property master to art director, first sweeping the set, then decorating it, then designing it. He was never a nine-to-fiver, much as I'd have liked on those long lonely nights that cropped up so often. He brought sand to the beach and trees to the forest. You didn't think the utopia in soft drink commercials actually existed, did you? Los Angeles air may be smoggy, but it is rife with illusion. Or rather, delusion.

Yet, as much as I knew about the parts, I still believed the whole. I cried at anything, everything. Books, movies, even commercials. I would stand behind twenty people on a tiny smoke-filled stage, watch them film an actress pretending to talk to her father on the telephone, yet still I would cry when the tender moment hit the screen. I was the perfect mark.

Perhaps that was part of the problem.

We agreed to stay in commercials, because movie work required too much travel and we didn't know many couples in that end of the business. Because there weren't many. Nope, I wanted him home. I want him. Home.

Halfway through my pregnancy, I forgot why I liked my job. Racking my brain twelve hours a day to spit out budgets — low enough to get the job, high enough to do the job — so Nike could sell more sneakers. The cool jobs were beer and cigarettes, which weren't really so cool when you rolled down your car window in the city and saw your success highlighting the existence of homeless families huddled in the alleys. Besides, I only pushed around the numbers. Those vast sums of play money gave me headaches and an ulcer. I did miss the paychecks, the power and dressing up.

Jim, like the rest of the hardworking folks who actually made the commercials and TV shows and movies, was freelance. You work, you get paid. You don't work, you don't get paid. You were lucky to work. And it was all or nothing: a month with no work, then suddenly all the production companies called at the same time. My theory was that the advertising agencies had to deplete their budgets at the end of each quarter. I'd rather our budget was more consistent, but I liked it when Jim wasn't working. He didn't play golf or tennis. He stayed home and surfed the waves of cable TV with his remote control. He'd watch anything with a horse in it. At low tide, he'd settle for men with hats. Either way, there were always good guys and bad guys and guns. He also read, a good example for Gina. Art, history, biography, mystery, he lost himself in books. But I always knew where to find him. So, he was the consummate escape artist: he created fantasy in his work, and sought it out in his play.

We floated from one paycheck to the next pretty well and we had what counts, which is true love.

I'm still not sure why he wanted me, out of all those beautiful women. Movable props, he called them. But they were there all the time. Every job had gorgeous models. They put suntan lotion on inflated breasts, eyedrops on blue contacts, toothpaste on laser white teeth. Then there were the non-pros, like this groupie from the music video. No doubt she was Hollywood hip in black spandex and red lipstick. I knew Jim, he was just doing his job, keeping bubbles in the bathtub. What nerve she had. I did trust my husband.

But you can't trust a woman in love.

5.

"Hollywood married." One of the main sources of entertainment in Los Angeles is star bashing. More delight is declared when celebrity marriages end than when they begin. It's the ultimate I-told-you-so of the commoner. Jim always said a year is typical when "monsters marry." He was generous.

My father, Moose, was anticipating his third marriage now, back in Ohio, so the disease was certainly not exclusive to the rich and famous.

My mother, Lois, travels around the country with the Del Monica Sisters, the famous over-fifty hoofers. She doesn't dance, but she did give up a thriving psychotherapy practice to be their manager. Mom was the black sheep of her family — they didn't believe in divorce. She didn't either, but once my dad had moved in with Wife Number Two, there wasn't much choice. Anyway, the gig got her out of the Buckeye winter and into show business, so to speak. Otherwise she would have followed me out here and suffered through the high cost of living on reduced HMO rates. As it was, she popped in whenever they passed through town. When they didn't, she called me constantly to impart her wisdom and keep in practice for when the arthritis killed their act.

Mostly, she was lonely. She was still hung up on Moose, or who Moose could have been. She thought he was her Prince Charming. You know what they say about love and hate. Now she's the dangerous one. But, enough about her. I'm sick of her life. I've lived it with her every breath of the way for way too many years. Thank goodness for Jim. Sometimes he'd handle the whole conversation. I couldn't wait until Gina was phone savvy — then she could take over.

The point is, around here, we don't even mention the D word. I'm against it. Think of all the marriages that end after eighteen years. Was it inevitable, right from the start? Did the husband and wife believe all those happy promises? Did they say the same things we said?

It's too scary. Does divorce invalidate the whole marriage? Does late pain obliterate early bliss?

Most of all, when do people start thinking about divorce? At what point does it enter the vocabulary of their consciousness? Does it start as a joke?

Those were some of the things I thought about when I swam laps. They were also the things that I tried to avoid thinking about when I swam laps.

So Jim and I decided early on. There is no divorce. The only D word around here is *death*.

6.

Staying at home has been both weird and wonderful. Having a child is all-consuming and it's a hell of a different world than I thought it was. Nine months seemed like an eternity — but it certainly didn't prepare a gal for motherhood. Fortunately, there were plenty of other moms and kids to hang out with. It was amazing how much you could have in common with somebody just because you were a mom.

Gina, of course, was the best. Spitting image of her dad in a delicate way. Strong legs and a belly soft as satin. She was quick, too. I didn't push academics on her, but she sang the ABC's in a haphazard kind of way at twenty months. It's absolutely inspiring to watch a baby become a person. And the fun we had! I loved petting zoos and pony rides and swinging and sandboxes. I got to be a kid again.

Sometimes, though, my imagination got the best of me. Gina, too young for much in the way of arts and crafts, hosted tea parties and played make-believe, but . . . I spent a lot of time imagining what Jim was doing at work while I was here supervising the development of our very own personal human being. I knew that a good baby-sitter could offer her love and security almost as good as mine, but I couldn't imagine anything more important for me to do. It was likely that this was the most impact I would have on another life, and the most important thing I would produce in mine, so I valued it dearly. Still, I got bored sometimes. Sue me.

Lately I noticed that I no longer recognized the names of musicians whose concerts inspired hysteria at the ticket outlets. At the kids' show at the mall I was not an old mother — but I was by no means a young mother. That flat-bellied girl in the bicycle shorts must have been the baby-sitter. I mean, that flat-bellied woman.

The bimbos at Jim's work were born when I was in junior high. Physically, I still felt young. Why wasn't I?

When Jim and I met, I was a younger woman — six years younger. I was surprised when I learned his age — he's one of those Marlboro Man types that make the suspender crowd pale in comparison. The difference seemed like a lot then, and I thought you married an older man because he had money — and I wasn't that kind of girl. So I married, obviously, for love. I loved the fact that he had already played around, so he was unlikely to follow in my father's footsteps. I especially loved the fact that I

26

would always be a younger woman.

I never considered that "younger woman" was a relative term. Who could be younger than me? At least if Jim had an affair, it would be with a girl in her late twenties. A woman, I mean. Wouldn't it?

7.

The phone rang incessantly. People looking for work in the Art Department, as if it were a real place. Jim almost always gave everybody a shot if they were persistent enough and he had a big enough job to use what he called a third broom. He figured if they wanted it badly enough, they'd give him a day for free just to get the lay of the land. Then if he liked them, he'd give them another day for pay. You never knew what talents you might find.

Like with Kim.

Most of the time, guys called for work. With so much production going to Canada, Jim had his pick of professionals. But he also got calls from kids starting out, with or without college or related work experience, and it was easy for him to use them. Someone had to carry those sandbags to the beach, and those trees didn't jump off the truck by themselves. Jim loved big strong young guys who guaranteed that he wouldn't have to lift much. Time being short on the set, and Jim being a perfectionist, he usually ended up straining his back anyway.

28

Girls were more of a problem. Women. They weren't all fit for heavy lifting: most were artists wanting to assist in the set design, or decorators who just liked to point. Even the fast shoppers didn't always have great taste, so the females were few and far between. Despite my concern about equal employment opportunity, this was fine by me.

I'd never been a jealous wife: Jim never gave me reason to be. Of course, I was jealous of anyone who got to spend time with him, especially when they got more waking hours than I did, but those people tended to be male.

Until Kim.

8.

You can tell a lot about a person by their phone manner. It takes a lot of balls to call a complete stranger and ask for work. So I always tried to be nice. If the caller came off like a jerk, you could bet that was the message Jim got. With all the time he spent on the phone setting up the game plan, he was happy to have an excuse not to return a call. He hated the phone. But if he missed a call or his beeper was off, he could lose a job. So when he wasn't home, I had to answer.

When somebody called who didn't treat me like a receptionist, I liked to be friendly and get the scoop. Kim was a sweetheart. She had just moved to town after getting a degree in theater from some tiny school in the Midwest. She had propped some local still shoots and sounded good. She was staying with a friend's cousin and needed work right away so she could get an apartment.

Kim was genuinely nice. I had to stop myself from inviting her over for dinner. Lord knows, we had enough friends on our dinner list — we didn't need to feed a stranger. Kim had gotten

Jim's name out of an industry reference book. I suggested that she memorize a street map of L.A., learn all the main vendors and call back later.

Jim is the kind of guy who'll spend his only day off in three weeks helping a friend move. I've come close to giving him an allowance to keep him from spreading his cash around to hungry assistants, down-on-their-luck friends and homeless women on the streets. I wanted him to keep his hands in his pockets. He believed that charity began at home. So did I; our home. It would be nice to be a few months ahead of our mortgage.

Anyway, I knew he'd give Kim a shot — I'd overheard him, calling around to see who was available for this big Kellogg's commercial. He was in town today prepping and he'd know his needs, as far as the job was concerned, by tonight.

Perhaps if Gina had taken five more minutes to fall asleep, I would have let the answering machine pick up her call. Perhaps if Jim hadn't been in such a good mood that night, he wouldn't have returned her call. Perhaps if fate's hand hadn't yanked us down this gentle path, nothing would have happened.

But it was my hand doing the yanking, wasn't it?

9.

There are always fireworks on the Fourth of July. Back in Ohio, cars drove around with mechanical bullhorns, waking the whole town in time for the parade. I wore my red and blue nylon racing suit and rode with my teammates on a huge flatbed trussed like a crepe paper barracuda every year until I was fifteen. After the tractors broke down and the Sno-Kone vendors ran out of ice, we had public races at Tremont pool. I always won the breaststroke, maybe because I didn't have any to get in the way. An ice cream social followed, which was just an excuse to run wild while your folks were busy drinking lemonade, gossiping with the neighbors. My folks had a few public scenes at that picnic, so the neighbors always had something to gossip about. I was too busy hammering rolls of caps and lighting sparklers to let it get to me then.

In Los Angeles, you have to seek out the Fourth of July. Oh, there are fireworks all over town, but you make your own holiday. Tradition always brought us to a friend's house high on a hill overlooking several city displays. Since

I had stopped working, these parties traced the lives of acquaintances I no longer saw, except on the Fourth of July. I'll never forget two years ago when a former film editor I was speaking to looked past me to watch her kids during our entire conversation. I thought she was rude. Now I know differently: children make you look past a lot.

Kim worked out on the cornflakes job, adding pastel pink flourishes to an immaculate high-tech white kitchen, a distortion of modern motherhood that the advertisers would have you longing for. Feeling sorry for this girl far away from home, Jim invited her to the annual blast. I looked forward to meeting her right up until the moment I finally did. Gina and I were eating ice cream, our favorite food.

"Audrey, this is Kim."

"Nice to meet you, I've heard so much about you. This must be Gina."

"Yes, hi." I started to extend my sticky hand for a shake, thought better of it.

She laughed. "That's okay. I'm not big on ice cream."

That should have been my first clue. "Oh. Anyway, hello, it's good to connect the voice with the face."

It was a nice face, a sweet face, a young face. And blond. Not the in-your-face bleach of your average bimbo, but a real, honest, unassuming blond. I wanted to like her.

Paul Minivitz stole Jim away to tap a fresh

keg. Kim watched him go.

"Jim is really terrific."
"Yup." I know. I married him.
"No, I mean . . ."
She gushed on, a fountain of adoration for my brilliant, handsome, kind, friendly husband. Suddenly, I didn't like this girl.

I remember being jealous before Gina was born, when Jim spent one entire Fourth of July party playing with the children. It was irrational and petty of me, but there it was. At least I knew he'd be a good father. He'd be there.

I tried to convince myself that this was the same harmless feeling. He returned as the sky was set ablaze with exploding light. Gina started crying from the noise. Jim handed me some napkins and took Gina in his arms to comfort her. I wanted him to take me in his arms, too. Instead, I put my arm around him, holding her. One of Gina's favorite words came to me.

Mine.

10.

The water was cloudy today. The pool man said we have too many dissolved solids and should drain the pool, but of course we couldn't refill it in this summer of drought. He said it wasn't to the point of being unhealthy, so I should just add more chemicals when I was through.

He was happy to have us as clients: he never saw anyone actually *in* the other pools he maintained. Oh, there might be some rafts and lounge chairs lying about. But never anyone swimming.

I took care to wear a swimsuit on Thursdays. Not that my incredible body would invite trouble, but as a polite precaution. He tended to show up at all different times. I wore an aqua blue tank suit that blended in with the water. I felt like I was a prisoner kept from my natural habitat, fenced out by a yard of Lycra. At least when I saw my belly upside down in the middle of a turn, I looked like I belonged.

I pulled on goggles to save my eyes from a day of uncontrolled tearing. Twenty years ago, we didn't wear goggles. My seventh-grade health teacher stopped short during her infamous manicure lecture to ask me how things were at home. It would have been a valid question had it not been provoked by my tears. My Visine habit, I assured her, was a proud reminder of the eighty-three ribbons pinned up on the cork wall in my bedroom. I stared at that wall for many happy hours. I wish I knew where those ribbons were now.

Soon after, glass goggles became popular. They were ugly black rubber things, only slightly smaller than diving masks, that made me look like a frog. One November morning, I sat on the starting block in lane 4 at the high school natatorium and happened to look at the clock. It was 6:00 A.M. I'd been up for an hour already to catch the car pool and had a lot of water to cover before joining another car pool to the junior high. I hated the school clothes I'd packed the night before, wasn't in the mood for a breakfast of V8 juice and granola bars and really did not want to be there. In protest, I smashed my goggles against the block, hitting the steel support bars. Some of the glass sank into the pool and settled to the bottom, where a synchronized swimmer cut her foot during practice. Coach was not pleased. At the afternoon stroke clinic, he didn't let me demonstrate my specialty, the whip kick. Instead, he had my well-endowed girlfriend do the honors. He let her continue on to the backstroke, but that, I recognized, was so he and the boys could watch her breasts loll back and forth. That night, Coach came for dinner to see Mom for therapy. He had lost his wife and sons over the head timer, a blond senior. He made me do fifty push-ups before dessert. After that, goggles got smaller and smaller until we were warned against removing them too fast for fear of sucking out an eyeball.

Now my goggles were state-of-the-art cushion-rimmed plastic in shades to match my mood. Red was a disturbing world to swim through, gray was slogging through the sewers, blue is vivid on a sunny day and clear was my favorite view of the kingdom I ruled under the ripples. If only I had goggles to see more clearly *out* of the water.

Jim stood over me on the diving board. He had to leave. I had to stop.

"What's wrong?"

"I have to go get Kim."

"I thought you had today off."

"I do. Her car broke down."

"Isn't there someone else she can call?"

"She called me."

"Why?" Why, why, why.

"I didn't ask her."

"She probably knew you'd drop everything and go." Unnecessarily flippant.

"I'd do the same for anyone."

"I know. Except it's not anyone, it's Kim."

"Audrey, is this a sexist remark, like it's okay

to help a guy, but it must mean something if it's a girl?"

Time to retreat. "I guess it is. Sorry. Will you be back to take Gina to the park?"

"I doubt it. I'm going to take Kim to that Filipino mechanic Paul recommended. You take Gina. Say hi to the moms."

"They only go in the morning. Your glasses are ready. Can you pick them up?" He needed stronger lenses for driving. I wasn't the only one familiar with Father Time. Except on him, it looked great.

"I'll try."

"Will you be back for dinner?"

"Sure."

"What do you want? I didn't defrost anything."

"Doesn't matter. If you make it, I'll love it."

Three hours later, he called. "Rudy says he'll have it finished in a half hour."

"Great, so you can come home now. Gina's asking for you."

"Well, give her a kiss from me. I'm going to stick around, just in case. I think he'll work faster with me watching."

"What happens if he doesn't finish?"

"I'll have to give Kim a ride back here tomorrow."

"Then stay, by all means."

"We'll grab a bite while we wait. How much do we have in the checking account?"

"Why?"

"I'm going to lend Kim some money. There's an ATM around the corner."

"Will she pay you back?"

"Of course, she's just broke right now. She didn't get paid yet."

"Neither did you. Okay, well, see you later."

"I love you."

"Yeah."

It sounded like he meant it. I guess I should have said "I love you" back. But he pissed me off, the Boy Scout. My mother said that most couples she saw complained about the very things that attracted them in the first place. I was attracted to Jim's generosity, and here I was bad-mouthing him for it.

But it didn't stop there.

11.

"Hello?"

"Hi, Audrey, it's Kim."

"Hi, Kim, hang on." I didn't even want to talk to her. Why waste my time? I knew what she wanted.

I found Jim stretched out on the big glider on the front porch, reading *Where the Wild Things Are* to Gina. I waved. Gina was engrossed in the colorful pictures of monsters. Jim looked up, concerned, mouthing "monsters" to me above her head.

"Those are good monsters, right, Gina?" Gina bobbed her head, intent on the story. "I'll take over. Telephone's for you. Guess who?" A real monster, I wanted to say.

Jim could tell what I was thinking. He gave me a look I recognized from when Gina colored all over the living room wall. We had never told her that this was unacceptable behavior, so we couldn't really punish her for being bad. Except Gina was quite a bit younger than I and perhaps more deserving of Jim's patience. He handed me the book and I quickly dove in where he'd left off.

They talked on the phone a lot. He was always giving Kim advice on her career, her apartment, her life. She was an avid pupil.

12.

No matter where you are or who you see, sometimes all indicators seem to point in the same direction. Do we seek out these aces to justify our weak hands, or does fate simply lay them open to us from a stacked deck?

Gina and I were going back to Buckeye country for my father's wedding. It was not the event that drew me, but the opportunity to see my old chums. I missed the rolling hills lit by stars, the old quarry singing with whispers.

Although I was not nearly a movie star, my stranded schoolmates always detected a spray of stardust when I returned, fresh from the lips of La-la Land. They had warned me about California years ago, when I left after high school. Even now, they didn't know the truth to those rumors of seduction. I love L.A., but I recently realized that, professionally, we were stuck here. Small towns suddenly had a new, inviting scent.

My old friends were dispersed over a fifty-mile radius of Middleburg. An hour away from Ohio State, giant buckeye leaves still adorn scarlet-and-gray garages housing red-and-silver cars. Go Bucks! Most of them didn't see each other anymore except when I invited them over. My father lost the mansion with his third marriage; this visit would require far more effort on my part.

Every woman plays a game of appearances. Before visiting people she doesn't often see, she buys a new dress, a new lipstick, a new hairdo. In the name of resurrecting the woman old friends knew and loved, she displays a new, improved woman, a woman that not even she knows quite yet.

"So, you want to impress the folks back home?"

"No, no, I want to impress me."

Ronnie, my hairdresser, scoffed. He'd heard it all. He knew better.

"So, how are things with Jim? When are you having another baby?"

How is it that an outsider brandishing sharp scissors every six weeks can get to the point so fast that you have no time to cover your bald spots?

"I don't know."

"What do you mean, you don't know. Trouble at home? Are you having an affair?"

If I wasn't so horrified, I would have pondered the inappropriateness of the question rather than the appropriate way to answer.

"Of course not!"

"Is Jim? Of course he wouldn't tell you, would he?"

"This is ridiculous. Can we change the subject, please? We will have another baby soon, you'll be the first to know, okay?"

Such power we give to strangers.

"I'm sorry, Audrey. I just stand here and listen to gossip all day long, and I tell you, real life is better than the soaps."

Ronnie went on to fill me in on the owner's new squeeze and the shampoo girl's latest bent, and I forgave him. He even offered to pull out my gray hairs. Ever the martyr, I refused. He was impressed.

I relaxed. Ronnie was the only one in town who could cut my bangs to look as good when I washed my own hair as they did when I left the shop.

When I returned home, flowers filled a dusty vase in the kitchen.

"For me?"

"No. For me." Jim shrugged apologetically without noticing my haircut. Typical. I sent him flowers once when we were courting. A daring and brilliant strategy that thrilled him into my arms. He was depressed, probably feeling the loss of his little black book, I don't know. No woman had ever given him flowers. I sent him daisies, my favorite happy flower with the smell of sunshiny weekends in endless picnic meadows. He started bringing me beautiful miniature orchids, fragile and expensive. I would have preferred daisies — or roses — flowers that smell. We continued to buy each other the blossoms that we ourselves preferred, until finally, politely, we leveled with each other. We haven't bought flowers since.

These were cymbidium orchids. How did she know? She knew. Damn. "She's after you, Jim."

"No, she was just thanking me for getting her work."

"For a girl who's broke, that's an awfully nice thank-you."

"She's a nice girl. And talented."

"And in love with you."

"Don't be ridiculous."

"What's so ridiculous? I'm in love with you. You are worth loving."

"I try to be." That smile again. He kissed me. I let him.

"I wish you could come home with us."

"This is our home."

Of course. My mistake.

13.

Stacy met us at the airport. She flew in from Atlanta with a twenty-four-hour pass from the network. She was a vision of sophistication until we went into the ladies' room. There, she cut a clean swath of cold cream through her on-air makeup and was back to being my little sister. No one who saw her newscast just before she ran for the plane would have recognized her. That, I suppose, was the best part for her. She oohed and aahed over Gina, but it took a while for her to really be comfortable holding her. Gina loved Aunt Stacy. She sent us videotapes regularly, so to Gina, Aunt Stacy was a celebrity right up there with Mickey Mouse and the Cookie Monster. Stacy had flitted like a firefly lighting up the airwaves from town to town so often that she hadn't had a chance to fall in love. Countless millions were undoubtedly in love with her — something we worried about with every celebrity murder story. She was, in full-dress regalia, a polished and stunning presence — anathema to the run-of-the-mill blond ex–beauty queens.

I was very proud of her. And a little bit jealous. I was supposed to be the smart one. There I was beating my brains out just trying to have a happy family life. But then I always found a twisted bit of comfort in the knowledge that her apartment, no matter how nice it was, was undoubtedly filthy. Beyond her seamless broadcast-quality appearance, dark hairs covered the makeup-stained floor of her bathroom. Her tub was ringed with ancient residue. Remnants of midnight yogurt splurges were crushed underfoot on her mildewed carpet. Her refrigerator was empty except for half a vacuum-packed bag of ready-chopped salad. Unopened bills cluttered every counter. Moving boxes were stacked in the corner, books were strewn on the floor, and the couch was a cache of current periodicals. Her TV and VCR were woefully inadequate, yet half a dozen police scanners tattled twenty-four hours a day. Her cat, Spike, left a black coat on every cushion. Mostly, the place would be flooded with clothes. Gorgeous and expensive anchor clothes that she was up to her ears in hock for. Before Atlanta, she'd had to wash windows for her landlord to make rent. Atlanta surely would change all that. Finally, a major market. Eventually, she would get around to paying all her bills and hiring a maid. Hell, she was used to towns so small that there weren't any maids for hire. It was time to cash in.

She ordered up a cushy rental car and took

us to lunch. Not that we didn't have friends or relatives that would have picked us up, but it was nice to have some independence. And we needed to talk. We were the close kind of sisters that would go six months without a serious letter, yet we'd leave blips on each other's answering machines recommending books. Mom always filled in the rest of the tape on both of our machines.

All the original restaurants in Buckeye country had turned into chains. We had our pick of places exactly like the ones we'd left. We finally went to a little café by the new mall. We were stunned to see Ann Taylor and Calvin Klein in a glass-and-chrome mezzanine surrounded by farmland. Such is progress. Gina was exhausted from her exciting flight and she slept through lunch. I ordered a large salad. Stacy decided she was on a diet and really wasn't hungry, then ordered a milk shake.

It was fun to see the Columbus corporate crowd on a regular workday. The colors and fabrics were more conservative than in L.A., but there was impressive evidence of style. Women dressed the same wherever. Rather, they dressed according to their stage in life.

"What do you mean?" Stacy didn't look serious with her strawberry mustache, but I could tell she was.

"See that woman with the short skirt and the jacket belted tightly around her waist? She's single."

"She could be married."

"Naw. She wouldn't have such high heels on. She's looking for love."

"She's dressed for work."

"Check out the redhead. Loose blazer, flattering but comfortable heels. Married but no children."

"How can you tell?"

"Her entire suit is made of silk. One wearing equals two trips to the dry cleaners. Plus all her accessories match, right down to her shoe clips. That takes time."

"Maybe she's just organized."

"Obviously she's organized. But look, her nails are perfectly manicured and very long."

"Maybe they're fake."

"I'm sure they are. That's a weekly appointment for fills aside from the major glue job every month."

"I don't think you can judge people like that."

"No? Next time you go to the pool, check out the women's toes. Singles have professional pedicures, marrieds do it themselves, new mothers give up altogether, old mothers splash on some color, then just let it chip for a few months."

"You're crazy."

"You'll see."

"Nope, I'm never getting married."

"Oh, come on. Don't let Lois and Moose steer you away."

"How can you call your own parents by their first names?"

"Okay, Mom and Dad. That just sounds funny in the same sentence, let alone the same planet."

"Aside from my old high school friends, you're the only one I know who's happily married."

Last time she checked, anyway. Oh, enough paranoia.

"But you put so much energy into it. I don't think I want to."

"That's what it takes, Stac. And it still doesn't guarantee anything."

"That's for sure. Boy, the affairs in the newsroom are awful. It's like these guys are such stars on the air, then they go home and their wives know they're just folks. They pretend they're mentoring the little news junkies they boff. Those gals are just looking to add names to their résumés."

"Does it work?"

"I swear, it must. Some of these kids hit it right out of school and here I've been busting my butt for years. I don't know how long I have to really make it before I'm too old."

"I think Atlanta is considered 'making it.' And you're not old." Hell, if she thinks she's old, what does that make me, besides three years older?

"I've followed my dreams for so long I have to look up my own phone number half the time."

"Some people don't ever follow their dreams. Some people don't even *have* dreams. You're lucky. Brave." I took a bite while she slurped her milk shake thoughtfully. I looked up at her, nonchalant. "People don't really have affairs like that, do they?"

"Maybe not. I hope not. I'm just feeling bitter. Maybe a little lonely. Here you sit, so happy and with that beautiful little girl. . . ."

"Everybody has problems." I didn't want to get into my own. She obviously needed some support. It was her turn.

"Yeah, but, I swear, I think you got the last good man."

I shrugged. I wasn't so sure.

"Oh, you know you did. You always had a steady boyfriend — a backlash to Dad, Mom says —"

"Of course."

"— but you broke it off so fast with that what's-his-name and married Jim. Like you knew."

"Well, I did know." Then. Now, I wasn't so sure. Gina opened her eyes. Aunt Stacy scooped her up and spooned her some ice cream. She was welcome to play Mommy for a while. I looked at my watch. "We better go before Dad thinks we missed our flights."

"Mustn't disappoint the groom." We laughed and gathered our things to leave.

14.

The wedding went smoothly. A bearded justice of the peace presided beneath a white wicker gazebo on a rolling expanse of public property on the green shores of the Scioto River. The brief, nondenominational ceremony was followed by a game of softball. It was a far cry from the ceremony at the St. Regis in New York City, where my mother made her big mistake. Number Three was close to my age, a nice enough woman, despite her soft spot for my father. Moose was into bodybuilding now, and looked better than he did playing varsity fullback his senior year at OSU. If you liked fully shaved senior citizens in bikini bathing suits, he was your man. An inspiration of aging ectoplasm. He was actually wearing a ring this time; my mother would insist it belonged in his nose. Now he says Mom was right all along: people are what matter. Small comfort to her now in that Ultrasuede motor home rolling down Route 10.

Moose and the missus took the train — after winning the softball game, of course — to some remote island on Lake Michigan. Moose was beginning to see his life as one long train ride, with pit stops here and there to exchange companions. He'd grab a woman in one arm and run down the tracks and hop back on the caboose, excited about a whole new journey into foreign territory. These treks were all long, with barely a breath between them. It was as if he were trying out different wives, a new life every fifteen years. He could never be reminded of past folly by a bride who hadn't been there, never see her plundered by gravity or even wise from the years.

I wanted to journey with Jim. I wanted to look out the window and admire the mountains speeding by. I wanted to know I was safe and sound and loved and skimming the ground along smooth tracks.

15.

It was a good thing I lugged Gina's car seat clear across the country, because we spent a great deal of time cruising. Stacy was on a return flight the next morning, after our short but sweet rendezvous at the theater of the absurd. So Gina and I were on our own. Ohio is quilted with ancient farmland, plenty of cows and horses to point out as we visited my childhood pals one by one.

Gina was a big hit, especially since most of the other children were older. They started young in Buckeye country: plaid blankets and hot cider didn't quite cure that post-football-game chill.

In high school, I was friends with an equal number of guys and girls, so timing the visits on workdays was tricky. Gina and I were early to see Buddy, who was in computer sales. Gina played with the new puppy while his pert wife plied me with Kool-Aid in a quest for Hollywood gossip. "Do you know a lot of movie stars?"

I shook my head. Work and restaurants didn't count.

Disappointed, she glanced at the television. "TV stars?"

"Sorry."

I followed her gaze. The early news gave way to a shiny bright Colleen, raving about some fabulous brand of — what? Hair color?

Buddy's wife interrupted. "Any celebrities at all?"

I tore my eyes from Colleen's face. Not a mark on it. But the slap still rang in my ears. "Mostly, I try to avoid them."

Buddy arrived and rescued us both. He looked pretty good despite the extra weight, de rigueur for married men there, proof of home-cooked lovin' or maybe just too much beer. I carried Gina along on a tour of the backyard, where he was putting in a scarlet-and-gray hot tub. Buddy had never been truly ambitious, but he had a real zeal for life. We used to skip study hall to cruise around town, listen to southern rock classics like Lynyrd Skynyrd's "Free Bird" and dream about our thrilling futures.

The first year of college, our friend Kevin was killed in a car accident with a drunken fraternity brother. Was he watching now? What would he be doing if he had lived? Then there was Will, who came home after graduation, put a large pistol in his mouth and pulled the trigger. Where is that line that divides restlessness from desperation?

Buddy couldn't understand how he'd ended up slaving away selling machines. Family life was fine, but he felt like he'd been cheated. How could his uncle be so happy changing city lightbulbs? That was all he did. By the time the bulbs on Main had burnt out, he'd be full circle from one end of town to the other, ready to replace them all over again, every eight months. He was the happiest guy Buddy knew. No expectations, no disappointments. Buddy complained to his white-collar father — no, after all those years it was more like a confidence than an accusation. He placed no blame. But nobody had warned him about real life. Wasn't there more? His father looked him square in the eyes and said, "Yes. Join the Shriners."

I smoothed back my gray hairs for the first of many times.

Some of my girlfriends there were happy staying home, staying even, unlike in L.A., where even above-average folks live with an awful anxiety to get ahead. It's a resentful angst born of the dangerous plethora of gilded Mercedes and beachfront mansions.

My closest friends had left town, like me, fifteen years ago, to chase rainbows and ambitions. Now that I think of it, the deserters were all children of divorce. Other friends talked about leaving; we left. We didn't follow the paths mapped out by our achievements but roads to rebellion and freedom.

Gina and I ran into Betsy in the drugstore.

She was a year younger than I, the breast-stroker who replaced me on the relay when I quit. Actually, she was one of the reasons I quit. She was now an attorney in the D.A.'s office. Most of the swimmers went to good schools and became professionals. There is some merit to the discipline required to swim six hours a day and still finish your homework. I asked Betsy if she still swam.

"I can't."

"What do you mean? You're burnt out?"

"No. In fact, I miss that private time. You know, the endless space for thinking and dreaming, and conjugating French verbs. But I can't seem to get in the pool — any pool — just for the fun of it. I have to do laps. And I can't just do a couple of laps either. I feel guilty if I don't go a mile. You know, what was it, sixty —"

"Sixty-six laps."

"Right. So I just don't do it at all." She stuck out her tongue, licked the inside of her forearm and smelled it. "I swear I can still smell the chlorine. How about you?"

"I still swim."

"No water on the brain?"

"Nope."

Not at all.

16.

Our plane circled endlessly. Over the years, I en-joyed aerial captivity less and less. A pilot once asked me if I'd rather be up there in the cockpit, given my absent skills. Smart-ass. How could I answer?

Marriage presents a similar dilemma. Is it safer to blindly take the lead or just to hang on the wing and pray?

I tried not to be consumed with doubt. I acted brave and sang Raffi songs for Gina. "Baby beluga in the deep blue sea. . . ."

I searched out the window for a landing strip. It was unreal. A three-dimensional Twilight Zone with no channel changer, no on-off button. It seemed the airport forgot about our late flight. They closed up and went home.

Will somebody turn the lights on, please?

17.

Morning. Gina was still sleeping off our trip when I went outside to feel the water, my water. Unpacking and laundry awaited me — the unwanted, unanticipated, unabating chore of married women. Jim followed me out, basking in my presence, I suppose. How could he miss me if I didn't go away?

I automatically picked up a dirty towel that had taken up residence by the steps. I tossed it onto a chaise lounge and stopped short. A pair of sunglasses lay by the pool. Silver wraparounds. I picked them up.

Jim coughed. "Your mother must have left those on one of her pit stops."

I looked up slowly. My mother? There were no gold-filled lions roaring from the temples or designer logos preaching from the rims. "Did she swim?" Like it would make a difference. Would it?

"She was never even here."

"Oh, really?" Funny how he knew exactly who I was talking about.

He took the sunglasses and got busy straightening up his bachelor debris. "They must have fallen out of my work bag when I was making notes out here. She left them in my car a few weeks ago. She forgot to pick them up when she came by the office to pay me back. Pay us back. Paid back every cent."

And more, I thought. "Funny, how she could forget something she needs every day. She must have been too dazzled by your presence."

"I guess she has a spare."

I had never seen Jim lie before. That's why it was so obvious. He couldn't aim those clear blues anywhere near me. He was backpedaling so hard he'd be in the water any second, unicycle and all. I knew what I knew, and I should have dropped it, but I couldn't resist the high-wire act. "Why did she even take them off? So she'd have an excuse to see you again?"

"Audrey." He refused to honor my accusation with a response. His avoidance was a flat-out denial. "So, you didn't say much last night. How was the trip?"

"I would really feel more comfortable if you weren't so friendly with her."

"Audrey. She could never hold a candle to you."

"That's not what I meant." Yes, it is.

"Yes, it is. You have no reason to be jealous."

That was true. She wasn't glamorous like the bimbos. I could understand the easy attraction of a femme fatale. It would be quick and nasty, an injection of lust. Kim was pretty, but no prettier than I was. Her figure was nice in an aerodynamic kind of way, but no better than mine. At least if she had big boobs, I could understand. But then, boobs were my obsession, not Jim's. No, there was no reason for my husband to want Kim. She was a lot like me.

Except younger.

I smeared lipstick into a smile to go to Thai Palace. The tiny room gave new meaning to the myth about a man's home being his castle. Garlic fumes warmed my doubts. I filled Jim in on places he didn't see and people he didn't know, then fell silent. We took turns helping Gina consume enough baby corn to justify the inevitable dish of ice cream.

Young lovers watched us with that familiar contempt of immature certainty that, unlike us, they would never run out of conversation. Often, Jim and I sat quietly on purpose, content to relax and dine in each other's company sans words. In peace. Tonight there was a wall of glass between us. A wall of distrust that I had built.

I was a million miles away when we made love that night. Sometimes you are so involved, Earth seems distant. Sometimes you go through the motions with the whole universe screaming at your back. I kept thinking she was here. The sheets were clean. Was she inside or just outside? But outside is my inside. Was the water forever tainted? Should we refill the pool, start fresh?

Am I sharing him? Did these hands touch her? Does he seem different? Is he fighting to keep my name at his lips?

He didn't notice where I was, or wasn't. Or at least he didn't mention it.

Am I that good an actress? Was I acting?

I couldn't sleep. I tossed and turned until Jim was snared between the sheets. He turned on the light.

The glass wall was still there, between us. I could see myself, three inches tall, in the reflection. I sat up and punched it. It shattered silently. Invisible blood on my hand. Splinters would fester for months.

"How can you lie to me?"

"What are you talking about?"

"You and Kim."

"Audrey!"

"Admit it."

"Admit what?"

"Are you having an affair?"

"How can you ask me that?" Hurt.

"I want to know."

"You're pissing me off."

Ronnie's words came back to me. "Would you tell me if you were?"

"Yes! I mean no. I'm not having an affair."

"If you were, you wouldn't tell me, would you? You wouldn't want to hurt me, right?"

"I am not having an affair."

"But you slept with her."

"No!"

I looked and looked and looked in his eyes and I wanted to believe him. Talk to me.

"If it makes you happy, I'll stop being friendly with her. She'd love to be friends with you."

"No thanks."

"She looks up to you."

I rolled over, away from him.

He turned off the light. We listened to each other's breathing. Audible angst.

"Do you think I should color my hair?"

I heard him sigh.

"No. You have beautiful hair."

"What about my gray?"

"What gray?"

I reached over him, flicked on the light. I pointed to my grays. He kissed them.

"I love your gray hair. And I'm not having an affair." He turned off the light.

"Jim?"

He was careful to sound patient. "What?"

"Thanks for not wanting to hurt me."

Jim shook his head like I was crazy, and maybe I was. He rolled over and fell asleep immediately. That pissed me off even more. Enough of this martyr business.

I shoved him. "Wake up!" I shoved him again.

"What?"

"Get out. I don't want you in my bed."

"Your bed? This is our bed."

"I don't care. Go sleep on the couch!" I pummeled him until he finally got up.

"I'm not sleeping on the fucking couch!"

"Oh, is that the 'fucking' couch? Then at least you know you'll be comfortable there!"

He glared at me. I goaded him.

"Won't you? At least you spared the bed!"

The words hung suspended in the air for a moment before they came crashing down on our heads. He grabbed his pillow and left.

I slammed the door shut. I sat on the edge of the thrashed bed, staring at the numbers on the digital clock across the room. When a minute passed, the number split in half horizontally and flicked under to reveal the next number. Digital implosion.

Footsteps shook the hallway.

"Goddamn it, open the door. I'm not sleeping on the couch."

I didn't answer. You made your couch, now lie in it.

"Don't ever hit me again, Audrey."

"Why, will you hit me back?"

Something light smashed against the door and scuttled to the floor.

"Open the door!"

I took note that he didn't call me any nasty names, nothing that would linger unspoken between us for eternity. He was a fair fighter. He wouldn't push me irrevocably away. Slightly appeased, I took up my position in front of the clock and turned on the radio. It was set to some incredibly annoying pop station, intended to wake Jim immediately in the morning and antagonize his senses so much that he would have to get out of bed to shut the damn thing off.

After several songs and a contest to win tickets for a concert by another group I never heard of, I found a nice jazz station.

The music mellowed me. I decided to let him apologize to me and get this whole thing over with.

I peeked out the door and called to him. No answer. How could he sleep at a time like this? I turned on the hall light. Jim's new glasses were mangled on the floor. A $250 temper tantrum. Served me right for marrying a Taurus.

I tiptoed down the hall. Gina was snug in her crib. Thank God she was a heavy sleeper. In elementary school, I could never sleep, thanks to the battles raging in my parents' room next door. The night before a science test I yelled at them to get a divorce so I could get some sleep. Things eventually fell apart after that. My mother blamed me for years. Christ, that marriage lasted seven years. The divorce took eight.

It will never happen to Gina.

I took a deep breath and tiptoed to the family room. The couch was empty. I picked up my pace and ran through the house. Shit.

The front door was open. His car was gone. Shit. Shit. Shit.

Oh well.

I stumbled back to the bedroom. It was too late to be at a bar. He would never air our problems with a friend. Not like I would, with my mother. The realization made me feel guilty. Betrayer of the betrayer. He wouldn't dare go to her house. Would he? He must have gone to a hotel.

I trudged back to the bedroom, turned on the TV. I found myself surfing from bad movie to bad movie. There was John Wayne, a comforting figure on a horse. Why was I doing this? I should have been watching reruns of *Love, American Style* on the other channel. I didn't want him to be gone. I wanted him here. John Wayne was close, but not enough.

There were two hotels nearby. A Marriott and a Motel 6. I called information for the Marriott's number. I should have looked it up, this would cost fifty cents. To hell with the fifty cents. Why was I worried about fifty cents when Jim was probably spending two hundred dollars not to sleep on the couch? I would have gone to Motel 6. Not Jim. After that scrappy youth living hand-to-mouth, sleeping on park benches and church pews and the stained carpets of whoever took pity on him, he'd be at the Marriott. His idea of camping was a hotel without room service. And we spent a lot of money on thick steaks and good wine. Jim was a Be Here Now kind of guy; fuck the past and who knew about tomorrow? Who? Not me, not anymore.

The receptionist confirmed his presence and connected me to his room. I wanted to hang up, but I was hypnotized by the hollow ring. He was not in. So there must have been a hotel bar open. I wondered if the bartender was a man or a woman. I turned off John Wayne. The darkness was empty. Sirens wailed in the lonely distance.

Jim's car lumbered into the drive — I knew it was him. I couldn't help running to greet him. Then I remembered why we had the fight and hung back.

He trudged in and slammed his keys down on the desk.

"I only came back for Gina. If something happened, you wouldn't know where to find me."

I opened my mouth to contradict him — then I changed my mind. He was home.

He went in the nursery to admire our handiwork. I hung back and watched him tenderly pull up her covers. Then I followed him down the hall to our room, to our bed. He stretched out on top of the covers, his back to me.

"Don't ever kick me out of bed again." A warning?

"You're the one who . . ." I didn't even want to talk about it. It had cost too much. More than the $450 to cover the hotel room and new glasses. I wanted it to be over.

He turned to look at me. I had a hard time maintaining eye contact. Why did I feel like the bad one?

I fought to keep from smiling, unwarranted mirth based on the relief. He waited until I looked right at him, then he pinned me.

"Can this be over now?"

"Yes," I said. But, no.

18.

Stroke, stroke, breathe. Stroke, stroke, breathe. Flip. Twenty-four laps. . . . Relentless. How dare the water not part for me? Out of my way, I must find that rhythm! But what good is a perfect solo rhythm? How can you tell it's perfect when it's a cappella?

Even a desperate rhythm is better, shared by two. If we were equally anxious we could plunge to the depths together and rise to an understanding.

I surely made a ripple in my husband's consciousness. But now he approached it as something I alone had to deal with, something I would eventually get over. He could not save me. He would tread water until I caught up.

25, 26, 27. . . This was not the answer. He was watching, waiting. I could not hide under the water.

He knew I would not divorce him. We'd spoken many times of the sharp incisions my father cut in my mother's heart. The scars were hideous, but they did not compare with the infection that spread each year as she pined for him. It was not worth it.

The other D word, then. It was the option most attractive to me. Once, when she almost succeeded in taking her life, my mother had seen a beautiful white light, just like rumor has it, and had been at rest. She was exquisitely happy . . . until the park rangers snatched her body from the Buckeye blanket littered with her usual picnic remains: a jug of wine, a loaf of bread, an empty bottle of pills. They dragged her back to life, where she lived through the purple-lipped, sallow-skinned shame of intensive care and a parade of too-late relatives expressing too little concern. No, not for me. I was already turning purple.

Could I kill Jim, the eyes that saw me in his big picture, the lips that kissed it good-bye? Yes, I could. Not in cold blood. I would study auto mechanics and fray a brake line before he left for a job at a distant location via the merciless freeways of Southern California. It would be an accident. His partner would break the news to me, his employer would be concerned, not that we had insufficient insurance coverage but that I might sue. But Gina would suffer; I could never do it. I didn't want her childhood to have any brush with death or the absence of love. It was upsetting that, at two, she already knew the importance of money. We needed it for ice cream, at the park. Perhaps it was unfair to keep children behind rosy glasses. The real world may blind them. But I will be there to

70

filter her light. So will her father.

Besides, he is a part of me. I need him. I love him. I want him.

Kim would be easy. We would have a barbecue. I would give her a cold but friendly Beverly Hills kiss in the air by her ear. I would brush her cheek with mine, comforted that it was equally soft, not framed by high cheekbones like Colleen's. Hers would be delicate with the moisture of youth, mine with the moisture of a religious, expensive skin-care regimen. In my innocence, I would give her a slim oleander branch to shove in her hot dog. It would be so appropriate, her favorite form. But then Jim had watched *Arsenic and Old Lace* on the late movie with me. He'd know it wasn't an accident. No, I didn't care enough about Kim. She should get down on her knees and thank whatever God she believed in that she was but a smelly speck of dogshit on my heel.

It was not Kim that I hated, although, okay — I hated her. I hate her still. But I hated myself for not keeping my husband happy, for getting old. Older than her. Why did he care about her? Was it the tantalizing allure of forbidden territory, her Bermuda triangle? How many men had been lost in such pristine traps?

33, 34, 35 . . . Each arm cut a swath through the water like the blade on a guillotine. I would catch up with Jim. We would find the same rhythm. I promised myself, I would get even.

19.

Jim used to be a swimmer. Not competitive, like me, but enough to be a lifeguard. Except he worked at inner-city pools as he whistled his way across the country. I worked at the Middleburg Country Club, with children from good families. I was not a member. I once loved a boy with a barrel chest, but it could not last. I was raised on the wide-shouldered, slim-hipped shape of a swimmer's body and would never have settled for less. Jim's blessed shape wasn't state of the art, but it was classic.

As for swimming, he was content with a dip now and then in times of extreme heat. And with playing games with Gina involving great feats of strength. She loved to be tossed up over the water and caught, splashing down like a lunar module. One more time. One more time. One more time.

If he insisted on treading water, then, damnit, I'd tread water with him. The current would sweep us away, together.

He would have to know. I wouldn't tell him, because then it would appear the petty game it was, once the layers of angst were stripped away like old lead paint. He would be tormented by suspicion until he could stand it no more. He would confront me and I would laugh. Or cry. It would be over.

I called Vic, my old boyfriend. He was a handsome devil with an eye for the ponies. The last time I saw him, we had dinner with his father at a rum-and-Coke rib joint on the fringes of Beverly Hills. The kind of place where ribs cost twenty dollars à la carte but the napkins were paper. The hostess bought him a drink he didn't order: he drank it. On our way out, the hussy slipped him a phone number he didn't ask for: he kept it. We had been monogamous lovers for years — at least I think we had. He tallied up orgasms with the same reverence and determination he gave the odds from his bookies, the ones he inherited from his grandfather. I couldn't believe his gall, accepting the blonde's advances, encouraging her by omission. He argued his case on the basis of naiveté and lack of intent, but I didn't buy it. Women always gave him the eye. He was a suave Sicilian, after all. Tall with white teeth gleaming from a crooked grin above the gold necklace I gave him that practically shouted, "Playboy — beware!" His father, who had been telling him to marry me for years, shrugged off our argument and left in a separate car. I never saw Vic again. It was not the specific incident that compelled me but the seed of distrust that it planted. Later he harassed me with petulant phone calls and the lure of a large, secondhand diamond scavenged from a jilted compadre.

By then, I had met Jim. Ultimately Vic convinced himself that I wouldn't have married him anyway. He teased me in letters that someday we'd meet by chance in a smoky steak house, ditch our spouses and have incredible sex on the carpet of the President's Suite at the Ritz. The Ritz sounded good.

I called his bachelor pad in Del Mar. I still got regular reports from friends who spotted him at the racetrack with a shadow of me on his arm. I wanted to stay friends — doesn't everybody? Like a fool, I had forsaken girlfriends, study time, work — everything that could possibly stand in the way of our time together. But, typical female, I still felt like it was my fault, because I hurt him when I broke it off. So I stopped sending postcards when Gina was born. She was so damn cute, I didn't want him to think I was rubbing it in. He answered on the third ring. A woman laughed in the background. I hung up.

This was too obvious. And dangerous. So much history to reinvent. Vic would enjoy it too much. Or he would be even more hurt. After six years, I had finally been with Jim longer than I was with Vic. Why upset the balance?

I wanted pain, not destruction. It was the difference between a splash and a tsunami. I would control this.

There were plenty of old work chums who might take me up on a fling. It might even be pleasant. Jim would find out casually. It would be like a mild earthquake that made you sit up in bed and thank God for safekeeping your relatively inconsequential existence. Plankton feeding off the surface of the galaxy. The last earthquake shook us awake on New Year's Day. The house shuddered . . . then the matching red bulbs on the Christmas tree all swayed in unison. Left, right, left, right, left, right. Nothing broke.

Maybe one of Jim's friends. Then he would find out for sure. He would forever be a cuckold. He couldn't show his face again in Hollywood. He'd stop working, surf all day in his black leather chair, lose the house, send me off to work and die of shame. Nope, it couldn't be one of his friends.

How about a complete stranger? I could pick someone up at a bar. I'd have to go to a bar first, which meant a baby-sitter or a good lie. And a condom. I wouldn't want to catch anything. We did want more children and I didn't want anybody dying of unmanageable disease. Condoms aren't even fail-safe. Then again, what is?

The phone rang, startling me out of my reverie. It was Mom, calling from Chattanooga. What did I think of Barbara Walters's new hairdo on *20/20*? She was wondering if Stacy should copy it, but still. Some people have stronger emotional attachments to news anchors than they do to relatives. I guess it's safer. TV pals rant and rave about death and destruction, but you're still fine, just inches away.

Real people could cause intense pain from a great distance.

"Hi, Mom."

"Hello, Audrey, how the hell are you?"

"Not so good." Suddenly wobbly. I sat down.

"Is my little Gina all right?"

"She's fine."

"Jim?"

"Jim . . . had an affair."

"Oh, Jesus, and I thought he was the only good man left. Then again, he is a man. At least he's not dead."

"Thanks."

"Did he tell you about it?"

"He won't admit it."

"Then how do you know?"

"He lied. It was obvious."

"Hmmm. Usually, when a husband has an affair, he does everything he can to make sure it's not obvious. And the wife goes out of her way not to notice. Even when it does get obvious."

"I guess I'm different."

"If only *he* was. I'm so sorry, honey."

Me too.

We fished through the silence for words.

"So, how is my darling granddaughter?"

If she had to change the subject, at least she picked a good one. "Great. We're working on potty training."

"How's it going?"

"Yesterday she pooped during nap time, took off her diaper and finger-painted on the wall."

"Very artistic. Takes after you, I guess."

"Did I do that?"

"I don't remember."

"Well, Jim was furious, but I thought it was hysterical. You know, like things you read about but aren't supposed to happen to you?"

"Story of my life, honey."

"Mine, too, I guess."

I could hear the Del Monicas warming up in the background. My mother's maternal grandfather was Willy Watson, founder of vaudeville's Beef Trust, a popular chorus line of fat ladies. He also gave Gypsy Rose Lee her start. So Mom was just continuing the family tradition. It was only a matter of time before she stepped in when one of the sisters got sick.

Mom demanded some new photographs of Gina and hung up. Moments later, she called back. "Was she younger?"

"Yup."

"Figures."

"Yup."

"How was your father's latest?"

"Big boobs."

"He told me she was a cheerleader at Ohio State."

"Figures."

"Yes."

"When did you speak with him?"

"He called me the other day. Oh, we're best pals now, he confides in me, almost like he's a real person." The unmistakable edge of sarcasm cut through her words.

"Life's just full of clichés, isn't it?"

"Well, honey, they wouldn't be called clichés if they didn't occur frequently in nature. Your father has deep problems. It would be easier for all of us if he would just die."

"I'm hanging up now, Mom."

"Someday Gina will hang up on you, too. Take care, honey."

I hung up. It was still nap time, which is tabloid talk show time. Who needs the *National Enquirer*, when these television hosts are the rich and famous equivalent to mud wrestlers? No offense to the mud wrestlers, they probably have fun and get a lot of exercise. I conquered my holier-than-thou principles and turned on the television. One show featured the New Monogamy. Wedding planners attested to the profits in this growth-oriented business. Young adults discussed their decisions to wed. It was truly romantic, seriously inspiring. Enough of this.

The rival show was about infidelity. Statistics showed that it happens more often than not.

Popular magazines said it could help a relationship. In Maryland, it was a ten-dollar misdemeanor. Here, in the land of no-fault divorce, there was a proposal to outlaw it. Comedians had a field day. Legal experts called it contrary to the First Amendment. Society is blasé.

I refuse to be crazed by adultery for the rest of my life. It's not so serious in the real world.

Only in mine.

20.

"Lara's Theme" chimed from the ice cream truck pulling up to the curb. The music was elegantly inappropriate. On weekends the truck circled the neighborhood at nap time, annoying mothers of light sleepers. On weekdays the truck could always be found here at the park. If only he would come after lunch instead of at 11:00 in the morning. It's no fun being a mean mommy.

Gina spent five minutes holding up the line to pick out a grape Mickey Mouse Popsicle. She dripped a purple trail back to the swings, but I refused to put her in until she was finished. Got to take our pleasures one at a time, sweetie.

The park was magical that day: no invasion of preschoolers hoarding the good slide, lots of toddlers with buckets and shovels to share. Other people's toys are always more fun. And other people's husbands?

The park is my element as much as the water. I have been immersed in park life for a shorter time, but perhaps with greater enjoyment. I love the water, but it is a daily battle for control. Gina offered daily battles, too — but I always won. I love you, but the answer is no. We giggled and laughed and played and hung out with the other mommies. An occasional daddy showed up, but the park belonged to Club Mom. The men made more money. The women had more fun, in a limited sort of way. What could you do, it was a fact of life.

When your whole life revolves around your family, threats are taken seriously. And dealt with harshly.

A single mom on her day off was playing with her infant under the tree. She was not the independent yuppie who wanted a baby. This young girl was more common. I watched her for a moment, silently demanding a reason for her suffering. I could have felt less awful if she was to blame — no birth control or something. Maybe she slept with someone's husband. . . . But that baby needed a good life. And the girl was a baby. If I'd had my wallet, I would have emptied it on her lap. I lashed on my emotional armor.

Gina found her friends; it was time to chat with the moms. We talked and talked and talked about things that college never prepared us for yet were suddenly of major importance to our lives — diaper prices, teething, birthday parties . . . eventually we turned inward.

Milena, an ex-lawyer who had perfected the

chignon, was unhappy in her marriage. We pointed out the positive things about her type A husband — like her exquisite wardrobe — and recommended a local therapist that she would never call. Cynthia, a young career-mom, wanted another baby, but her husband wasn't ready. Since the birth of Hannah, he wasn't even interested in sex. She colored her hair a different shade every week, hoping to make some difference. We assured her that more time would be a good thing. Diminutive Kathy, formerly a nurse, had to fight her husband off every night. Was the national average really three times a week? That must have been couples without children. We spoke about the sex and violence inherent in childbirth. We relished the romantic antics of our favorite celebrities, but we never crossed the line to divulge our own.

This was not a group to confide in. My crisis would threaten the sanctity of every life on the playground.

The kids wandered over to the plastic jungle gym. We dashed over to protect our babies from a misstep four feet off the ground. Who would protect us?

"Will you have a face-lift?"

"Excuse me?" Milena caught me off guard.

"A face-lift. You know." She stretched back her crow's-feet.

"Jim says wrinkles are the prize of experience." It popped out of my mouth.

"That's sweet. But it only holds for men."

"It's expensive."

"So? You don't think it would be worth it?"

"I don't know. I've never thought about it." I was too busy worrying about my gray hair.

"Well, think about it. A lot of the actresses are getting them in their thirties."

"They make their living off their beauty."

"Don't we? Our husbands support us." Milena glanced over to the group of nannies supervising several children.

"Thank God we don't need BMWs to be happy." Cynthia.

"I'd be happy with a new BMW. A convertible." Kathy.

"Not enough to go back to work."

Children laughed in harmony all around us.

"Naw."

"Do you put on makeup before your husband gets home?" Milena was persistent.

"Never! Okay, sometimes a little mascara. It used to be always, but . . . my sister told me I'd be less vain once my attention was diverted to a baby. She was right."

"Stacy doesn't have kids."

"No, but her friends do." Did, I should have said. The ones who used to be her friends. Unlike the ones who used to be my friends, the single career women. We had all the wrong friends.

Milena cleared her throat. She didn't care

what my sister thought. "So, all day long, our husbands see women put together in nice clothes, high heels, full makeup —"

"They're not all pretty."

"They're not all ugly. A lot of them don't have children. They still have their waistlines, and they're —"

"Younger."

"Right."

"They won't want to support us if we look our age? What about the children?" Cynthia.

"All I'm saying is that youthful looks are attractive. Men are attracted to beauty."

"My husband loves me."

"Call it an insurance policy."

"You aren't giving any credit to the men!"

"Do they deserve it? Historically speaking, that is?"

"You're talking about Jack and Drew and Wade and Jim. They're good husbands. They're not going to go out and find a younger woman because of a few wrinkles."

"You read too many magazines, Milena. They stay in business promoting that crap."

"Audrey? You're awfully quiet, suddenly. What do you think?"

"I'm afraid of needles, I don't think I'd like somebody cutting up my face." A good nonanswer.

"You're avoiding the issue."

I shrugged. So what, I was avoiding the issue. I was living the problem.

Gina ran over to me. "I want wunch, Mommy."

"Lunch, baby, you mean lunch. I need a big hug first." She wrapped her body around my chest and I hid, squeezed inside a moment of joy. "Thanks, cutie. I love you."

"Wunch, Mommy!"

Kids. Always to the point. And a great excuse to end the conversation. We spread out our blankets and dozens of politically correct re-usable plastic food containers and traded off string cheese for applesauce, peanut butter for turkey and mayo.

"Will you keep an eye on Gina for a minute? I'm going to get a drink."

"Sure."

I waved to Gina. She was occupied with Cynthia's homemade cookies. Our kids called the other moms by first names, because that was what they heard us doing. At this age, should we confuse them with formal titles? I don't think I'd know to answer if somebody called me Mrs. Hastings.

There was no line at the ice cream truck. Without the distraction of Gina, I actually looked up to order. A shirtless young man read Dante's *Inferno* behind the wheel. He had a chest like Jim's — before it started slowly sinking south — before I knew him. Young green eyes swung from the bowels of hell to me. I smiled. The ice cream man tore his shirt from

85

the chair and pulled it on to serve me properly.

"You back for seconds? Want some candy?"

Never take candy from a stranger.

"I get it, you're a dentist stirring up business."

He laughed, a cool, confident, attractive laugh. A young optimistic forgiving laugh.

"Your father, then. He's the dentist. You put his card inside every candy bar." Friendliness was an easy distraction.

He came over to the open door. He pulled a bandanna out of his Levi's and mopped a sheen of sweat from his neck.

"Retired Air Force. If he was a dentist, I wouldn't be here."

"What do you mean?"

"I'm a grad student. Not much money in ice cream, but I get a lot of reading time."

"I'll have a diet anything."

"You don't need diet."

Flattering, but presumptuous. I glanced back at Gina. She hadn't missed me.

"I like diet."

He pulled the tab on a cold can, handed it to me, smiling an apology. I accepted.

"You must like kids."

"Seven sisters."

"Oh, my God. How's your mother?" I had trouble comprehending the reality of eight children.

"She's great."

"Are you the oldest?"

86

"Youngest. I've got a dozen nieces and nephews." He opened one for himself, offered a toast. "Here's to moms."

I couldn't refuse. We clinked cans. I reached up to put my change on the counter, counted out pennies. I was short. He put his hand on mine.

"It's on the house."

"No, thanks, I . . ." I pulled my hand away, groped deeper in my pocket, nothing. My money was back in the diaper bag. Damn.

"Okay. Thanks."

"My pleasure."

I walked away, strangely self-conscious. I felt his eyes grazing across my shoulder blades, probing down my spine, marking a path around my hips for future reference.

Or was it my imagination?

Milena looked up when I returned to safety. "What took you?"

"I forgot my money."

"I have money. You can pay on the way out."

"No, mine's in Gina's bag. I'll catch him later. Thanks, though." Why was I embarrassed to admit I got a free drink? Did I really believe they'd be jealous over a seventy-five-cent freebie?

He reminded me of Kim. Maybe I should set them up.

21.

A fly buzzed at the darkened window, trapped on the wrong side of freedom. He landed on the sill, watching us in the split lenses of his eyes, like a bank of TV screens tuned to the same channel. Yet he saw us not at all. We sat close, an intimate and complementary pair, worlds away on the printed page. Jim was roping steer and saving pioneer women on the Ponderosa. I was in Bali, sailing an uncharted course. The calm water erupted into furious froth, marking a treacherous course ahead.

I dropped anchor in the depths of my escape and swam back to reality.

My water glass beckoned me with condensation that streamed slowly into a pool on the night table. I grabbed it, but it slipped from my hand and spilled onto the bed. Jim looked up. He moved away from the spreading pond as I rushed to lay a towel down.

"Looks like I have to sleep on the wet spot again."

He smiled, put down his book. We hadn't spoken much since the night before and I could tell he was searching for a safe subject. "You taking Gina to the mall tomorrow?"

"Nope, I've had about as many puppet shows as I can take for a while. Plus, I always want to buy her everything in the toy store."

"Why don't you?"

This, in a nutshell, is the basis of the good cop–bad cop act played by every money-conscious middle-class mother and father in America. I didn't legitimize his question with an answer. "I think I'll take her to the park." I knew I'd take her to the park.

"I thought you went to the park today."

"We did. We like the park."

"I can tell."

Could he? What could he tell?

He picked up his book. He was not suspicious. Couldn't he read my mind tonight? Didn't he want to? He felt me watching him. He looked at the clock, put down his book.

"I have to get up early."

"I know."

"Good night."

"Good night." He flung the covers off and sprawled out to sleep. On normal occasions, I would have huddled up close to him for body heat with the covers carefully pulled up to cover me but not touching him at all. Not this night. I turned around and scrunched up in a ball, like Gina did when it got cold in the early morning and her covers were wadded in the corner from a round of midnight acrobatics.

22.

The ice cream truck was not at the park when Gina and I walked up. We got out her sand toys and went to work. I wished I was not so disappointed. It seemed silly to be distracted by an ice cream man. Ice cream boy. If it had been a successful executive, perhaps the competition would have been fair. Or should I say, he would have been a more obvious threat to Jim.

But this boy did remind me of Jim. When he was younger. How I imagined Jim was when he was younger. Did Jim have an eye for older women then? I knew he once broke up a marriage. He didn't know the woman was married. Then again, I am not sure that he ever asked.

So this was perfect. I didn't need a real rival; this whole thing was not about Jim, after all. It was about me. Kim was a younger me. Why shouldn't I have a younger Jim?

Gina wanted to swing. I picked her up, swung her up to the sky to touch the stars, then settled her down into the canvas seat. She squealed and clapped her hands.

"Two hands, cutie, two hands." Such a good

girl, she clutched the sides. She swung back and forth, back and forth. Laps in a swing.

"You want down now?"

"No! More!"

Was there a magic number for her, too, one hundred swings to happiness? No, she just loved to swing. I admired that gleeful face, those rosy cheeks, those bright eyes. Defying gravity. I envied her simple pleasures.

"Lara's Theme" tinkled over the loudspeaker as the ice cream truck approached. My heart beat a little louder. I looked around at the other mothers. Did they hear it?

"Ice cream!" Brilliant child. "Ice cream, Mommy."

Nonchalant. "What's the magic word?"

"Peeese!"

"Okay." Bad Mommy. I helped her out of the swing and stalled her with the practical task of putting her socks and shoes back on until the line disappeared. I didn't want to be obvious. Just adulterous.

What a fool was I?

23.

"Hi. We'd like a yogurt push-up today." I whispered, "She thinks it's ice cream."

His green eyes were the shade of seaweed that entwined my ankle and dragged me into the undertow. It was easy to con a mother: be nice to her baby. "What's your name, pretty girl?"

"Smart girl," I admonished. I didn't want her obsessed with looks. Not like me. Heaven forbid.

He came down the steps to offer her the treat. Gina hid behind my skirt, typical. I took it, handed it to her. She accepted it eagerly from me.

"Is she going through that clingy stage?"

"No, she's just shy with men." Smart girl. "Her name is Gina. Short for Genevieve."

"That's quite a name."

"She's quite a girl. Plus, my husband's a romantic." Oh, my God, just what I didn't want to talk about, my husband. I had to say something quick. "I'm Audrey."

"Sean. Nice to meet you."

"Well, I appreciated the drink yesterday."

"The diet drink." He smiled.

"It was a hot day."

"My pleasure. I enjoyed talking to you. Usually, the mothers are so busy with their kids, no one even looks me in the eye."

A shame. It was a hypnotic experience. "Yeah, well, ice cream can be very stressful for a parent."

He laughed. His Adam's apple danced up and down, playing peekaboo behind his collar.

"How's hell?"

"Excuse me?"

"Your book. Weren't you reading the *Inferno*?"

"You know it?"

"Intimately." The word stuck in my throat. I swallowed it, embarrassed. "I still have the Cliffs Notes."

He acted innocent. "Maybe you could help me. You ever go to the beach?"

"Gina loves the beach." We both looked at her. She was a sticky mess.

"I'm house-sitting for a friend in Malibu. Why don't you come by sometime?"

Milena's car pulled into the parking lot. She got out and waved. I waved back. "Sometime, maybe."

"Tomorrow, for instance."

"We'll see."

Sean glanced around at Milena's approaching eyes, retreated back up the steps into the truck.

Joshua careened past on his plastic fire truck. Gina followed, dumping the remains of her push-up.

"You're getting soft in your old age." Milena is a year older than me. The comment, especially in front of Sean, irked me.

"Shut up."

She laughed. "No, I mean, ice cream two days in a row."

I pulled some napkins from the dispenser and turned away from the truck to mop up Gina's mess. Milena had stopped at my side.

"She ate all her oatmeal this morning — the kind with one hundred percent of the Daily Vitamin and Mineral Requirements. And she had broccoli last night."

"Don't be defensive, it's okay by me." We walked together to the shady benches on the edge of the sandy playground. "I thought you'd be at the mall this morning."

"Nope. Too nice out. How was it?"

"Awful. You were smart to come here."

Was I?

24.

The next morning, I packed up Gina's sand toys, her diaper bag, her lunch, towel, sunglasses, lotions, extra clothes and whatever else I could think of that we might possibly miss in a variety of circumstances and was ready for the trip. Children require a lot of baggage. They also help to create some.

I put the car in reverse and stepped on the gas. Crunch. Oh, God, I hoped that wasn't a sprinkler head. I handed a toy to Gina and got out to look. I had driven over her toy boat. It was a big blue and yellow tugboat that tooted when you pushed down the smokestack. Jim gave it to her and she adored it. This was not a good sign. I snuck out of Gina's line of sight and buried it in the trash can. I would replace it later and no one would know the difference. I felt like a traitor.

But I got back in the car and drove Gina to the beach.

25.

Topanga Canyon Road is a black snake hissing through the coastal mountain range. The canyon itself is a country refuge pocketed between the suburban sprawl of the valley and the sapphire waves of Malibu. It is a ten-mile pocket of liberals who cling to septic tanks and kitten-fed coyotes in defense against the commercial success of designer tie-dyes. The location is a lifestyle choice, not unlike modern marriage. You pick your choice and you stick with it. Or you pack up and move on.

A well-dressed woman passing through in a convertible Mercedes braked on the curve ahead of me, chatting dangerously on a car phone. That could have been me. Another choice I made. Am I too old to have that someday? Do I still want that someday?

I fought the urge to yank the steering wheel, speed off the cliff into the ravine. It wasn't quite so tempting today, not with my precious Gina in the car. I turned on a cassette of Raffi, Gina's favorite singer, and took a deep breath. Bridges evoked the same feeling. What if I just turned the wheel and drove off, plunging into the water below? What if, what if, what if . . . Would my family miss me, or would they think I was a fool? Would I feel the warmth of my mother's white light? Gina would miss me, Jim would be burdened . . . besides, what if I survived with irreparable pain and damage? Not worth it.

The last curve opened to puffy clouds bouncing on the horizon like beach balls above a rainbow of catamarans. We descended to the parking lot. A girl in a yellow wet suit whizzed by leaning back from the mast of a sailboard. The wind whisked her sail over a big wave and then died, leaving her stranded. She stood, waiting to sink, then jumped off on her own recognizance. She kicked hard to push the heavy board past the breaking waves where she could try again. Excuse me, I wanted to yell, could you watch my baby? I'd like to try that. I bet I can do it. Maybe I can do it. Oh, forget it.

I scanned the weathered porches embracing the beach. No Sean. I dumped Gina's buckets and shovels onto the soft sand, but she ran right down to the water. Fearless. I followed and held her back from leaping right into the sea. She squealed as the cold surf licked her toes. I lifted her up when the next wave threatened and set her down when the tide retreated. We played this game over and over and over and in her joy I lost track of ulterior motives.

"Boo!"

I screamed. I snatched Gina from the hungry waves and looked around. Guess who.

"Sorry. I didn't mean to scare you."

Then why did you say "boo"? "It's all right. Hi." Another bad omen. Why didn't I just go home then, quit while I was behind?

"You look great!"

That was why.

"You and Gina, too, a real vision of womanhood, mother and child, so happy."

So happy. I deflected the compliment. "She's a good girl."

"I can see that, but I mean both of you — you too. A real Madonna portrait, and I don't mean the pop star. Everything a man could want."

Which man? I smiled demurely.

"I'm glad you made it."

"We always come to this beach." Not always. Did I want to do this, or not?

We sat down on the blanket. Sean helped Gina make a sand castle. Rather, he piled it up, she stomped it down. She was having a wonderful time. Like a postcard, addressed to my husband: "Having a wonderful time, wish you were here." Except Jim hated the beach. He liked the ocean, hated the sand. Not much room in there for compromise. He used to take me, way back when, but now his free time was more precious and he was more stingy about it.

If I made a fuss, he'd take us, but then I'd owe him.

After a few years, everything you do in a relationship has a certain point value. It was a constant battle to stay even. That's why I was there.

I was glad that I wore this simple tank suit. I bought a new bikini this year, but that seemed too conspicuous. It was red. I wanted to be subtle in my infidelity, as if it was a spur-of-the-moment, casual fling rather than a premeditated, vindictive betrayal. Which was worse?

Sean was wearing baggy trunks that emphasized the hard symmetrical lines of his stomach. My dad thinks tight is sexy, he should get a clue. Then again, most men find tight clothes sexy on a woman — they also find them cheap.

Good wives struggle to find clothes sexy enough to keep their husbands interested but not so much as to attract anyone else. It's a losing battle, so we ultimately dress for ourselves, which we should have done in the first place to save wear and tear. Rumor is that feminists dress for themselves; feminine women dress for men out of guilt and a need to please. But a need to please grows out of the desire to please, a product of free will if there ever was one. How can feminine and feminist stand for two such opposite sides? They are born of the same word! They are the same woman!

Perhaps men are more simple, more one way or the other, more black or white. Macho or sensitive. I don't think so. They just keep it to themselves, like everything else. I once asked my fourth-grade teacher, Miss Dean, what was the difference between boys and girls. She was an exuberant, if strict, young woman fresh from the Up With People musical tour. Her pale face puffed up like a tomato and she said if I didn't know by then, she wasn't the one to tell me. A penis hung in the air between us, yet that wasn't what I meant at all. At the time, I believed there was no other difference. Now I know better. That extra chromosome, the organic inequality of hormones, makes every difference. We are as unlike as two members of a common species can get.

Gina collapsed in my lap. I gave her a bottle and stroked her hair. No wonder my cat hated me. Gina was so much more wonderful to pet. "So, I brought my Cliffs Notes."

"Great. So far I can't get around Dante's concept that hell is for those who choose it."

"Sin is a choice. Dante assumes that people are aware when they choose to sin." A dangerous subject. Wasn't revenge a sin?

"Then I guess it's the definition of sin that I'm having trouble with. In my family it was a sin not to stand up for yourself."

An easy out. "Sisters, I remember. I guess it was a relief when you finally arrived."

"For my father. The girls pretty much ignored me, into their own things."

"It must have given you an interesting perspective."

"Like they say, the toilet seat was always down in my house. Did you see that new TV show last night about a family of women?"

"Excuse me? Last night?"

"Yes. My cousin is one of the writers."

"I must have read about it. Sounds like a fun job. Does she like it?"

"It's a he."

"A man writes that show? Were there a lot of car chases?"

"It was pretty action-packed. But it seemed accurate to me."

"You're a man."

"True. It wasn't the kind of show I'd watch if it weren't for my cousin."

"So, you're saying it was a woman's story that would only interest women because it's about women — even though it was written by a man."

"Right. My sociology professor says that society is always seen from a man's point of view, so it's like that's how life really is anyway."

I shook my head at the thought of such a dinosaur influencing a generation. Did Sean agree, or was he testing me? "I read a book last week, written by a woman in the point of view of a man."

"Wow. Did it seem like a man wrote it?"

"Yes. I really believed this jerk, Harry, needed to sleep with his brother's girlfriend."

"Sounds well-written."

"It was, but for other reasons. After all, if everything in society is from a male's point of view, what was the challenge, really? And even though I believed in Harry, I still didn't understand why it had to be her."

"So you didn't get the benefit of a woman's supposedly more advanced emotional considerations."

"Exactly."

"Audrey, you are a fascinating woman." He leaned over and kissed me. I let him.

"I'll bet you say that to all the girls." Girls? I felt young, dangerous. And stupid? No. I should have, but I didn't. I felt powerful. Supreme.

Gina rubbed her eyes. "I better get her home for her nap."

"She could nap here."

I followed his tan, firm arm past his pointing finger along a row of cliffside cubicles to a cottage on stilts above the sand. It was lovely, a perfect location. I looked down at Gina's slumbering face. She looked like an angel. So sweet. So innocent.

"No, thanks. She likes to wake up in her own crib." Not in a strange house with a strange man with her strange mother. I stood up.

Sean started gathering toys and towels.

"You don't have to do that."

"It's okay. Can I see you again? Here? I'd really like to get to know you better. You could help me with Dante."

We both smiled at the shallow excuse. I would help him learn about sin, he would help me commit it. Partners in crime.

26.

48, flip–push off–kick, 49, flip–push off–kick, 50
. . . I was a swimming machine today, equipped
with sonar. Hollow pings bounced off the walls,
resonating through my shiny mass. The water
put up no resistance, my steel arms tore through
it. The water surrendered and changed sides. It
clung to me, a second skin.

Jim read the newspaper on the redwood
chaise. Sweat dripped down, streams across his
reddening skin. He refused to put on lotion, a
sissy thing. Newsprint covered his fingers as he
turned to the next page. He read every word of
every paper with total concentration. I'm sure
he was aware of my presence, yet I was not
there, because he was somewhere else. He did
not respond to newscasters like my mother did;
he saw them as overpriced mouthpieces, talking
heads. He cornered Stacy with political history,
pushing her toward excellence whether she
liked it or not. He wanted the details, the guts,
the experience of the world that he retreated
from. He did not think to probe my mind, to

question my actions. I had grown — or perhaps shrunk — to be part of the framework of his life. He did not question it. He thought everything was fine.

Why would he think otherwise?

Jim was the rare man who listened yet the typical man who didn't ask. My constant stream of musings was old foil wallpaper to him: he spotted himself in a reflection now and then but didn't see the anguish in the flocked velveteen. He said he liked my gray hair, so I should be satisfied or I should color it if I was not. Yet, he was the prodigal son of our culture — how could he see past the gray? He was humoring me, flattering me with compliments from the book of husbandly etiquette. But the gray was not solely a change of pigment: it was a challenge to life as I knew it. He thought I was silly, and vain, a lightweight. I was all of those things. More.

Midlife crisis is a common term for men who buy red race cars when they go bald, and sleep with young blondes when their wives are tired. Middle-aged women just hike up their drooping breasts and keep going, painting over the grays one by one until they give up altogether and become little old ladies rocking beside supposedly wise old men. Or they become slaves to the scalpel and deny the inevitable. Women have no publicly approved crisis: we mature faster, harder, withstand stress and childbirth and longevity and are simply designed to hold up. Right?

It starts so early — before early — when male sperm swim so fast and burn so brightly. Fireworks. Female sperm, with that extra chromosome, are more patient, more understanding, more hardy, more responsible — all those things boring and necessary to create and sustain lives so the men can go out and swim so fast and burn so brightly and end so quickly.

Breath by breath, I saw Jim disappear and return with Gina. She was a water baby, anxious to play.

Jim sat with her on the steps, filling plastic cups.

64, stroke stroke breathe, flip–push off–kick, stroke stroke breathe, flip–push off–kick, 65, stroke stroke breathe, flip–push off–kick, stroke stroke breathe, head down touch the wall, 66!

I join them, relaxed, recovering. Done.

"You were really moving today."

"Yup." Away from him.

We hadn't spoken of Kim since that night. I was above it. Or at least equal to it.

Equal rhythm, opposite directions.

27.

After circling the vanity mirror, shrieking crows flapped their wings and finally planted their feet around my eyes. I had never heard their cries before. I scavenged the cluttered drawer for cover-up, dabbed it carefully in the tiny welts. More eye pencil, more mascara.

"You look nice."

Of all times to notice. At least he didn't ask why women wear makeup to sit in a darkened theater. It's not for the escort: it's for the competition on-screen. The preservation of ego.

"Thanks. I'll be back by ten."

"What movie are you going to see?"

"Whatever's playing when we get there."

"Have fun."

I plan to, sucker.

28.

Sean opened the door before I knocked. His sandy hair grazed the archway as he led me inside and kissed me. The games were over. Let the games begin!

The fiery sunset slipped down the sky through the open balcony of the tiny apartment. The heavens melted in crimson streaks on the horizon. Champagne sparkled in a crystal goblet on the balcony. The bubbles sang my name.

We stood at the edge of the world, my world, watching gravity drag all innocence down beyond the open sea. Surrender to darkness.

Sean nibbled the back of my neck, under my hair — was my weakness so obvious? I shied away, a hypocrite, to memorize the face of my demon pawn.

He was gorgeous, every woman's fantasy. But he was no harmless dream. Pleated pants hugged his smooth stomach tightly, caressing young hips then falling loose, teasing the outline of his flanks. Tufts of copper peeked above his starched white shirt. His deep-sea eyes sparkled above the taut cheeks of a recent shave. All of this for me.

"You are so beautiful."

"Do you have a thing for older women?"

"You're not that much older."

"I am. Eons."

"I've never met anyone like you. I've never loved anyone like you."

Uh-oh, the L word. Easy, now. "You mean you don't pick up mothers as a rule?"

"No. As a rule I don't. But you're not just a mother."

"Wait a minute, what's wrong with just a mother? What does that mean, 'just a mother'? There is no 'just' with 'mother.' People don't appreciate mothers. You should, eight kids. Geez. People think that once you're a mother you're tapped out of potential, it's the children's turn. That's just not true. It's an inferiority-based reaction from men."

Sean laughed at my outburst. "You are an incredible woman. So many women all wrapped up in one."

I turned to the twilight. "You hardly know me."

"I have this feeling about you. Still waters. You fit into every landscape so easily, yet . . ."

"And where do you fit in?"

"You tell me."

He led me to the leather couch and refilled my glass. I have always loved champagne. It's a holiday in every sip. Even the glass is special, a flowering flute or hand-etched goblet. I like holidays, any excuse for a celebration, an escape from the norm. I knew what I was escaping from. I was uncertain what I was escaping to.

Sean raised his glass for a toast. I lifted mine up and clanged his, too hard. I heard the crack of contact and imagined deadly sheets of leaded crystal crashing to the hardwood floor, slivers slicing through guilty flesh . . . but only pale liquid sloshed out. I was absolved. I looked around for a cloth to wipe up my spill. Sean propped my glass upright, set his down beside it and caught my hands together, palm to palm. Shall we pray?

"Just relax."

I took a deep breath and tried. But my adrenaline was pumping and my nerves were tingling and my lips felt flaky and dry. I breathed. I swallowed. My gaze swung to the sky.

The stars were exploding like bursts of Morse code, sending me a message. I tried to decipher it, but a shooting star arced above the dark water and I rode the tail until it disappeared.

Sean sat close to me. I groped for conversation. Sean's lips sealed mine to silence. I shut out the blinding starlight and kissed him back, sinking into his pillow lips. He released my mouth, infiltrated my neck. The confusing path from head to heart. My breath grew heavy and my limbs grew weak. I let him press me backward and I pulled him down, down, down into my underwater cave.

Lost in longing, the world was far away. Down here, the water swirled around me, a warm whirlpool of sensory delight. Cool air pricked at my shoulder as my blouse fell away. Waterlogged, I didn't resist. Soft lips covered my naked truth. Sean stretched out, hard intentions pressing against me, bursting my liquid cocoon.

"You feel so good."

My eyes flickered open, Orion hovered above, hunting for me. Shut up, shut up, shut up!

"Your husband's a fool."

Orion reached down from the heavens through torrential currents to my lost soul, yanked me violently to the surface. I pushed Sean away, gulping the harsh air. I wanted to vomit.

"He doesn't appreciate you."

Maybe not. But what would be left to appreciate? I stood up, wobbly. He beckoned me, my hunter-gatherer, my conscience, my husband. God, I hated me. I pulled myself together, grabbed my purse.

Sean stood up, his hard-on insulting and real. He'd crossed the line. He shouldn't have gotten personal. No, it was personal. Too personal. I didn't want to be on his side of the line. I wanted to be back on the safe side. I wanted to go home.

I didn't trust myself with the cliffs of Topanga: darkness would seduce me, guilt would propel my leap. I took the freeway; I was free. The pass between the mountains into the valley was clogged with smoke. I looked for the fire, the emergency sirens wailing for me to pull aside, let them pass. Help was on the way. But the shroud was fog, a dense hangover of the marine layer, following me. I chased the silent parade of taillights, red with shame. I tunneled through the mist until the glittering valley filled the windshield, celebrating my escape.

Safe!

29.

I slept in a tiny ball that night, fending off a migraine. Jim stayed up late watching a festival of Westerns. I was glad to see him so happy, so easily pleased. I love him so. I was still upset about Kim, but maybe I understood. Maybe, with men it wasn't so personal. What was I saying? I knew it was. I refused to understand. Why be superior about understanding something that causes you only grief, regardless? Jim may be foolish, but he is not a fool. We're still on the same train, watching the world whiz by. So what if we hit some bumps now and then? I wasn't trading him in. He was home, husband, father, man. Mine.

A new patch of grays had cropped up on the back of my neck. Sean left them there. All that time, those expanded lifelong days, I thought he made me young. I cooked waffles and bacon and the three of us, my family, had a cozy breakfast in bed. My affectionate kisses were taken as a truce to start anew.

I cleaned up the kitchen without a complaint — why fight it? Jim helped to clear, but it was still my unwanted responsibility. I felt the old resentment crowding my happiness, so I rebelled once again and went for a swim. No one could take this away from me. Except me.

I dove into the sparkling water and coasted as far as my arms could stretch. I was not in the mood to swim laps today, hurray! Such a load off my mind. So what about those gray hairs. The sparkle of my diamond ring lit the water in front of me. I spread my wings and flew down along the cool bottom, a pterodactyl with bubbles streaming up from my flaring nostrils.

I came up for air then dove back under, rolling around in my amniotic sac of chlorine comfort. I let the natural gravity of my buoyant mass lift me to the surface, then I rolled over to enjoy the view of the clear blue sky. A canopy of leaves waved to me as I floated on my back. Maybe it was time to give Gina some company. When I looked down, my naked hipbones framed the future.

Suddenly, a grenade exploded near my temple. Just when all was right with the world, I was attacked by apricots. That was the problem with fruit trees. Everything ripened at the same time. How could you handle it all? Most ended up rotting on the ground, a juicy haven for bugs. Gina, at least, would be thrilled.

I heard laughter from the porch. Jim unlatched the white picket gate for Gina and grabbed the skimmer net. Gina peeled off her diaper and stretched out her arms to me.

"Catch me, Mommy!"

She jumped to me with a splash and I swung her around. Her giggles made my heart sing. Jim skimmed around us, tossing the apricots into the brush. I grabbed hold of the long pole. "Why don't you come in, darlin'?"

Of course, just then the phone rang. Jim pulled away to go inside and answer.

"Isn't the machine on?"

He shook his head and went inside.

"Wait! Use the portable." We finally got a good one to avoid somebody cracking their head open on the wet concrete.

Jim heard me, came back out and picked it up. He stared at it, trying to decide which button to push. He finally figured it out, said hello. He shrugged, put the phone back down on the patio table. "Hung up."

I thought nothing of it. "Come on in, the water's great!"

"Come on, Daddy!" As usual, Gina had the most pull. Jim eased in, wincing at the cold.

"Lightweight!" We splashed him and he splashed back.

The phone rang. "Your turn."

I flew Gina over the water into his arms and climbed out to answer it.

"Hello?"

"Audrey." Sean.

I hung up quickly, too quickly.

"Audrey?" Jim looked at me. I shrugged.

"Another hang-up." I slipped back into the water, but, for me, the fun was over.

115

30.

The next week, Jim and I were ships passing in the night. I was a freighter, riding low in the water, heavy with unclaimed goods, awaiting a tugboat to drag me to a clean berth. He was a polished cruise liner, visiting dozens of tightly scheduled ports.

He had regular pit stops at home between long drives to and from the desert location up by Edwards Air Force Base. The commercial was for a pickup truck that had to burst out of the TV screen onto the road, then drive away. He and the special effects wrangler created a giant candy-glass window set at the end of a ramp for the stunt driver to burst through.

I swear, those advertising executives just sat around smoking cigars, dreaming about pink elephants flying. Then Jim had to figure out how to paint those damn elephants and get them up in the air. There was never enough time and never enough money, despite, or maybe because of, the so-called creative folks' gourmet dining habits. In L.A. it is no sweat to spend five hundred bucks on dinner à deux.

These connoisseurs traveled in hungry packs. Then, when the work was done and Jim collapsed into bed for three days with an aching back, a blistering sunburn, and two-inch calluses on his feet, the agency folks patted each other on the back for a job well done and took their first-class flights back home to show off their work.

I felt like a single mother with a part-time bed warmer. I needed him to be home now, to regain the intimacy necessary for our lives to continue and for recent digressions to vaporize. But Jim's needs were more immediate: uninterrupted sleep, clean socks and Levi's, coffee filters and espresso for his morning jump start. So I waited. I left the answering machine on to catch Jim's work messages between hang-ups. Gina had a cold, so it was a good excuse to avoid the park. We watched videos and played games with her little "guys" — the miniature plastic figures of every cartoon character known to man. Finally, her nose stopped running green and we went to the zoo.

The zoo was always better coming than going. We pretty much tried to hit the highlights: the elephants, zebras, bears and giraffes. One of them was always inside its cave, escaping from the bees descending on the ice cream cones and churros clutched by small sticky hands. It made me angry when we drove all the way there for the ideal zoo experience and missed it by one or two animals. If I said,

"Let's go see the hippo now!" the hippo would be asleep behind some boulder. Today, the rides were closed. Another hazard of rising liability costs. Insurance, the monopoly of extortion. I'll never make promises again. It was frustrating to have to disappoint my honey girl, so I clammed up in the interest of not raising her expectations. Perhaps that is a reasonable guide for parenting overall. Instead of helping the children look forward to good things, open for a fall, happiness could be introduced as a series of random surprises.

By the end of the morning, I felt sorry for the caged beasts and was relieved to go home. Gina took a while to soak up all this exposure and fell asleep in the car, overwhelmed. Once we were home, she couldn't stop talking about the elephants, displaying renewed interest in her animal coloring books and stuffed mammals. The zoo was easier to appreciate in retrospect. Most things are.

The next morning, Gina was still high on the zoo. She got down on all fours and lifted her arm like an elephant's trunk. I cut out some floppy gray ears and pinned them to her headband and she was in heaven. Which gave me an idea . . . after nap, I took advantage of her mellow spirits and dragged her to the mall. Oh, she loved to shop, don't get me wrong, but only if the trip concluded with a tour of the toy store. I was ready to indulge her today. I had but one hit on my wish list, Holiday Wigs. After all, if Gina could be an elephant, I could be a blonde, right?

I told myself I would not go so far as to bleach my hair — I was confident in my beauty, just not my age. I would stick with brown out of respect — and self-righteousness. But I just wanted to check it out. What would it feel like to be blond? Once on *Oprah* the entire staff went blond for six weeks. Aside from tremendous upkeep, all of them loved it. Only one would return to her roots. I can't, for the life of me, remember why.

Gina was every bit as excited as I was about trying on wigs. The saleswoman wasn't so thrilled, so she kept after Gina. This was ideal, of course, because between my polite, earnest smiles, I had the wigs and the mirrors completely to myself.

I dove for the long blond head, the Styrofoam siren pawed by hundreds of other customers, designed for thousands of men. It felt funny, hot and kind of stiff. I certainly looked different in it, and I felt different as well. I tried a vacant stare with my wide fake smile. That looked appropriate, but I felt awful at being so sexist myself, laying into the whole stereotypical myth of dumb blondes. I wasn't into the myth; I was into the reality. Blondes attract men. I glanced out the window. A handful of men passing by ogled me. Usually I have to at least smile to get that reaction. No need to dwell on the obvious. Blondes do get more attention. But is it the right kind of attention? And, more important, do they have more fun?

I yanked the wig off my head and groped for the next one. Nope, I was not a shag kind of gal. I lifted up a glossy pageboy, a sleek and soft model of golden threads. Ah, that looked nice. I'd have to lighten my eyebrows, but it was classy. Hold on — classy? I could be classy as a brunette. What I wanted with blond was joie de vivre . . . youth . . . my husband. The pageboy was great, but it wouldn't do. The short bob was too trendy, the short-short too drastic. I found a beautiful upswept do crowned with golden ringlets like Cinderella. Now, I felt gorgeous. An elegant halter dress — or a pink gingham apron — and I was local royalty. It was a bit of a stretch from my usual ponytail. A tough sell for day-to-day living. It wasn't the point of being blond.

Gina started whimpering, and I saw Madame Holiday had her in a scissor lock, a red Afro at her feet. Perfect excuse for escape. "Gina, honey, are you all right?"

"Ma'am, she was in —"

"I understand," I condescended. "Sorry about that. Thank you."

"Perhaps another time?" Wishful thinking flew like arrows shot after me out the doorway. I flashed a big fake smile and gummed Gina on the neck until she screamed with laughter. On to the toy store. I was feeling magnanimous. I had solved the blond riddle. I would not grovel to it. There was another way to save my marriage, and I would find it. I would make him want me again, not a blonde, not anyone else.

The toy store in the mall had a small doorway for the kids to walk in and a tunnel to crawl through if they were so inclined. The play area was well-stocked with indestructible toys and pint-sized playhouses. I liked watching the moms cruise the aisles while the kids tore the place apart. They should have a sign over the doorway, MADNESS REIGNS HERE.

After forty-five minutes of concentrated browsing, I bought Gina some small, easy-to-hide birthday presents and lured her out with a new bucket and shovel for the park. It had been a while. It was time.

31.

Kids from day camp swarmed the park, like ants on a Pepsi spill. Teenagers blew whistles with newfound authority and herded their wards into color-coded groups on the softball field. Gina watched, rapt, while I led her through the maze of children to where her friends played in the sand. The moms were all there.

"Where've you been, Audrey?"

"Around."

"Not around here."

"Got sick of the park. Gina had a cold, anyway. Hi, Cynthia. You cut your hair off!"

"Drew hates it."

"Men always like long hair."

"I thought it'd be a refreshing look, you know? Clean and —"

"Young."

"Now, Milena, don't start."

My turn. "I was thinking of cutting my hair, but my new hairdresser said it was the last time I could have long hair."

"I don't get it." Cynthia bit the plastic wrapper off a hunk of string cheese.

"Because I'll be too old. Or maybe it won't grow back so fast anymore, I don't know." I didn't know anything anymore, that I was sure of.

"Hair grows until you die." Milena, the voice of authority.

"That's what I thought. Anyway, it pissed me off. I'm looking for a new hairdresser again. Bangs or no bangs."

"Audrey, didn't you just switch recently?"

"Yup. I'm looking for someone to tell me I'm gorgeous and make me feel that way, too. They're all just too honest anymore. But I do like yours, Cynthia."

"It doesn't matter, it backfired. Drew was shocked that I would cut off my hair without consulting him."

"Like it's his property. Like you are."

"Milena, shut up."

Men do seem to like long hair. Jim and I met when my hair was earlobe length, the shortest it's ever been. But since I grew it out, his famous last words to me on the way to the hairdresser are "Don't cut too much!" As much as he likes my hair up, to see my face, the glory lies in hair that falls freely down a woman's back. Men.

"Well, I think it looks cute."

"I do, too. Besides, it'll grow."

"Milena!"

"Sorry. I'm torn between stopping men from usurping all this power and just going along

123

with it to keep things simple."

The ice cream truck chimed into the parking lot. The children perked up and studied us to see if we were game. Cynthia sighed.

"You guys up for ice cream today?"

"Not me." Never again.

They all followed my lead and joined the sand castle brigade at our feet. That's one of the best qualities of toddlers — they are still easily distracted if you try hard enough. After a few minutes, another little girl raced by on her tricycle and her mother ran to catch up before they got near the parking lot. Gina looked over to watch them, saw the truck again and remembered.

"I want Sean, Mommy."

"Shhh, no, baby." I downplayed her request and pressed a bunny mold down into the sand. The kid had an incredible memory. Gifted, my mother said. What a time to see it in action.

"Sean?" Milena. Who else?

"Is that the name of the ice cream man?"

"Yup."

"I didn't know you were on a first-name basis with the guy."

"We see him all the time, what's wrong with knowing his name?"

"Nothing, I guess."

"Okay, here's the scoop." Dour faces at my bad joke. "I was trying to get ice cream on credit the day I forgot my wallet, so I made nice with the kid. Okay?"

They accepted my alibi and the incident crumbled into the sand. We were a new breed of penny-pinchers who scoured the papers for the weekly pull-out flyers from our favorite discount stores. We looked forward to saving money on items that we could otherwise do without. Most of the stuff was for the kids: videos, clothing and earthquake supplies.

I looked heavenward for respite and noticed a gray cloud edging toward us. The wind started whipping up the sand and sprayed it over the children. Gina must have felt me watching, because she looked up just in time to get some sand in her eyes. She started bawling, so the other kids looked up at her and got sand in their eyes and soon everyone was upset. By the time the moms had all claimed their sobbing toddlers and calmed them down, a few drops had sprinkled.

"Anybody hear the weather report?"

"Sunny and fair, three percent probability of light showers."

"Three percent is looking large at the moment."

All at once we dove for our toys, shouting over the wind to see who owned the green rake and who owned the pink watering can, and shoved everything into bags. I found Gina's sweatshirt in the stroller and pulled it down over her head. The Girl Scouts have nothing on us with that Be Prepared motto. Moms take those words to heart with Baby's first spit-up. The others bundled into their minivans and offered us a ride. It looked like it would take them ten minutes just to get settled in their cars. We lived pretty close, so I just jammed Gina into her stroller and got moving.

I entertained Gina as Mother Nature cried from above, her wet despair enveloping us in a cold, dark cloud. I sang "Singin' in the Rain" and was just starting the elephant march from *The Jungle Book* when lightning cracked. Gina was frightened and started crying, so I picked her out from under the hood of the stroller to hug her close. Thunder rolled past us and the skies opened up, drenching us both before I could put her back underneath the canopy. We were a block from the park, but still a good five minutes from home.

"Lara's Theme" twinkled in my head and I thought I was imagining things, but a muffled honk behind us convinced me otherwise. Sean pulled up and waved for us to get in. I looked at my little girl, shivering. All I needed was for Gina to get pneumonia. Her defenses were down from her latest cold, so even the refrigerated ice cream truck looked like a good idea.

I handed her up to Sean. No matter what I thought about him, I did trust him with children. I didn't waste time compacting the stroller into a flat puzzle, I just jammed it through the open back door and climbed aboard.

"Thanks."

"My pleasure. I saw you leave. I've been wanting to talk to you." He handed Gina back and I hugged her tightly.

He turned the engine on and pulled away from the curb. I leaned unsteadily against the locked passenger door. There was no seat there. I was wet and uncomfortable and grateful.

"Please don't call my house."

"Why won't you talk to me?"

"It's over, Sean."

"It didn't start, Audrey. What did I do wrong?"

"Nothing. Look, it was a mistake, that's all. Nothing against you."

"I need to see you, Audrey. I won't take no for an answer."

"You have to, Sean. I'm a married woman."

"So?"

"Doesn't that mean anything to you?"

"Why should it? It didn't mean anything to you a week ago."

"That was different."

"Why?"

I covered Gina's ears. "I just wanted to get back at my husband for having an affair."

"That's a lie. You came on to me. You wanted me. I could feel it."

"I was just being friendly." Gina twisted free.

"Bullshit."

"Please don't swear in front of my daughter."

"Sorry." He reached behind him into a box

on the shelf and gave Gina a pack of Chiclets. She was delighted with the colorful package and the prospect of candy. It was gum. Jim didn't allow her to have gum, it was choking food, he said, but I was not about to make an issue of it at this very moment.

"Look, Sean, I'm sorry if I hurt you. I should never have . . ." I gave up.

"I broke up with my girlfriend for you."

This was news.

"Why? I mean, I didn't even know you had a girlfriend. It's not my fault. Three days of knowing me and you —"

"What if I love you?"

"Don't."

"We're great together, Audrey. You can't just drop me like this. This isn't high school."

I couldn't believe he said that. I mean, that was why I'd stopped this whole thing. I tried to explain. "Look, you have to take responsibility for your life. That's what I'm doing. And I can't afford to have you in it. I have too much to lose."

He turned on my street before I had a chance to point it out. Goose bump time.

"How do you know where I live?"

"I looked it up. You're in the book."

I was a bit taken aback, but then, it was public knowledge. We pulled into my driveway. Thank God Jim wasn't home.

"You can't just ignore me, Audrey. I always get what I want."

"That's just because you were the baby in the family."

He smiled, having finally gotten a rise out of me, personal contact. He stopped the truck and I tossed the stroller out onto the lawn.

I stepped down carefully with Gina. "Thanks for the ride. Good-bye." I waited for him to say good-bye, but he just turned and faced front, setting that straight jaw so firmly that his cheek muscles flexed.

I hurried away, into the house. I locked the door, convinced that my premonition of doom would pass along with the rain.

I ran a warm bath for Gina and peeled off her clothes. Things were settling down with the steady pitter-patter of rain.

The front door burst open and I screamed.

"Hello! It's me!" Jim. Thank God.

"In the bath!"

His head brushed against the doorway and he crouched all the way down to give Gina a kiss and then me. "I didn't mean to scare you."

"What are you doing home? Not that I mind it."

"The shoot got called on account of rain."

"But it just started raining."

"It hit us out in the desert about two hours ago. I've been on the road fighting traffic ever since."

He could have been here at any time. "I'm glad you made it safely."

"Thanks, darlin'. I have to make some phone calls to rearrange the schedule, but maybe we could make a fire? Drink some wine?" He looked at Gina, splashing happily in the bubbles.

Romance or family time, which would it be?

"And juice, of course."

I nodded. Family time sounded good to me.

"What was the stroller doing out in the yard?"

I forgot about the stroller.

"I put it in the garage, but it's going to need some airing out tomorrow."

I nodded. No problem. Anything.

Jim went to his office in the back of the house and I sweet-talked Gina out of the tub into her fuzzy pj's with the elephant on the front. The elephant's trunk was an extra flap that she liked to lift up. She had worked up to a darn good elephant imitation. I read her a book, wound up her musical lamp, and she was conked out in a second. So much for family time. It would have to be romance time.

If I could just clear the cobwebs from my head, I could look forward to this. Maybe a hot bath for me, sure, that was the ticket. I got a packet of violet suds for Mother's Day, it was perfect. The only bath accoutrements we stocked anymore had Big Bird on the label. Since becoming a mom, I'd learned to appreciate those little toiletries that used to make such boring gifts. The tub emptied with a gurgle. I recapped the drain and turned the hot faucet all the way up. This would be good. I went to check on Gina to make sure she hadn't kicked off the covers.

The doorbell rang. I rushed out of Gina's room to shut her door against the noise. My stomach curdled at the fear of who it might be. It rang again and I decided not to answer it. Maybe Jim wouldn't hear it. If only the intruder would stop before the noise woke Gina up. I stood there, stewing over what to do: ignore it, or put a stop to it?

It rang again. Jim rushed past me and opened it. My heart stopped beating for an instant.

It was Elvis.

Well, actually, it was my mother in an Elvis mask. She turned and waved the taxi off. I hadn't even heard it pull up in the rain. Headlights painted a bright stripe across the house as the taxi backed out. I noticed a partially drenched suitcase at her feet. Jim laughed and opened the door wide for her grand entrance.

"Oh my God, it's Elvis! Reincarnated as a woman!" He leaned down about twelve inches to hug her. She pulled down her mask.

"Mom! What are you doing here?"

"Oh, I thought it was time for a visit. I haven't seen my Gina in over a month. Where is she?"

"She's asleep."

On cue, we all start whispering.

"Oh, darn. Well, I guess I'll wait." Jim laughed and pulled in her suitcase, an old Louis Vuitton held together with duct tape.

"Hi, Mom." I bussed her warm cheek. "What's with the Elvis impersonation?"

"Oh, I met your sister last weekend in Memphis and I just couldn't resist. Isn't it a gas?" She pulled it clear off and admired it.

Jim shook his head. "Elvis in a skirt, who'd a thunk it?"

32.

Jim lit that fire and opened the wine he had mentioned, but romance didn't fill the air the way I'd hoped. My mom was always good for some laughs until I got sick of her, and this time I wanted her out of the house in short order. She and Jim talked endlessly about obscure books while I poked at the smoking fire. The logs were still damp from the rain that had seeped into the woodshed. I jammed a marshmallow on the barbecue tongs and roasted it until it crumbled in a heap of ash. I love toasted marshmallows — dark and crispy to the touch, white and gooey to the tongue — I lacked the patience for mere browning. Each time the confection caught fire, I was too dazzled with the swift consumption of flame to blow it out in time. The hard black sides slid off into the fire, where they quickly turned to ash.

Melodious babble wafted in from the nursery and we all smiled at each other, pride bursting from our breasts. Then we raced to Gina's side, fighting over who would pick her up, who would change her diaper, who would give her juice. Gina was a little afraid of Grandma at first, a living legend from the photos. When your age is still counted in months, two of them is a long time between visits. After a few minutes, she reached out to Daddy, still staring at Grandma. Once I gave Mom the juice bottle, Gina had warmed up and was eager to go to her.

Mom offered to baby-sit while Jim and I went out to dinner, but Jim was looking forward to a home-cooked meal. Which, of course, meant that I had to cook. Jim cooked for company, with a cotton diaper over his arm, and he was a good cook, but it was all for show and dinner was never ready until after ten. I give him credit for doing all the barbecuing, but he burned everything by not waiting for the fire to die down. We learned to love it that way. Mostly, he was just too pooped to cook when he got home late, and when he wasn't working he didn't feel like cooking either. He was a modern kind of man in theory, not in reality.

Mom raved over every bite of pasta, as if that would make it more fun, but really she was just tired of Caesar salads on the road. After coffee, she put Gina to bed. Jim cleared, which was nice even though he feigned ignorance regarding the location of the dishwasher. He would lay the plates on top of each other, with the silverware in the water-filled bowls. I had to reach in the grimy soup later on to retrieve it all and put it in the dishwasher. Thank God we had one.

Hondo was playing in 3-D on Channel 5, a special event, so Jim's evening was well in hand.

"I have to go to the post office."

"Now?"

"I forgot to send Stacy her Elvis T-shirt."

"I don't think Stacy wears T-shirts, Mom."

"She wears everything I send her."

Uh-huh. "The post office is closed."

"It's all ready, I just need to drop it in a big box."

"I'll do it for you in the morning, Lois."

"Thanks, Jim, but I've got an itch to get out anyway. How do I get to the post office?"

"Take a left out the driveway, another left on Capistrano, right on Oxnard, then left at the third light. I think it's on Erwin."

Mom listened politely, but her face was a blank.

"Lois, would you like me to draw a map?"

"Mom, go to Macy's, take a left. Turn right at Saks."

Her face lit up with understanding. "You want to come along?"

"You mean, will I drive you?"

"I can drive, honey. I know exactly where we're going."

"That's okay, Mom, I'll drive."

Once ensconced in the privacy of my car, I

put it to her. "Why are you really here, Mom?"

"Because I love you and I wanted to see you."

Maybe. I cocked my head at her. She nonchalantly peered out of the passenger window. She felt my skeptical glance.

"Because I missed Gina?"

Acceptable, even expectable — but not the way she said it. "The truth."

"I'm worried about your sister."

"Stacy?" Not me?

"You got any other sisters I don't know of? Never mind, don't answer that. There could be bastard children all over the country for all I know. On second thought, he must be sterile."

"Let's not talk about Dad, okay? Why are you worried about Stacy?"

"She needs a good husband."

"The world needs a good husband. Stacy knows better."

She gave me a pained look. "I think that's just an act. She doesn't give any man a chance."

"She's busy, Mom. She wants to get where she's going before settling down. I mean, who knows where she'll end up?"

"She'll end up alone."

"She will not. Lots of people get married later these days. I just read that twenty-five percent of men in their early thirties are single."

"That's men, not women. By forty those men are married. To younger women. Don't argue with me, you're living proof. Women don't get married later."

"Serious career women do."

"I don't think this has to do with her career. She has a problem with intimacy."

"Oh God, here it comes."

"Don't you talk smart to me, you know what I'm talking about. You were there when it all happened. In reaction, you gave up a lot to hold on to your man."

"No, I didn't. I didn't have anything yet."

"Well, you would have. You do now."

Our eyes met, but I didn't want to talk about it.

She sighed. "Your sister has taken the opposite approach."

"Vive la différence."

"This is serious, Audrey."

"Mom, with you it's always serious. Stacy's not a baby anymore. Whatever effect . . . things . . . had on her, she makes her own decisions. She doesn't want to be tied down when she has no idea where she'll end up!"

"If she got tied down she'd know where she'd end up."

"And personally, I don't think she's met the right guy yet. When she does, everything will change."

"No. She doesn't give anyone a chance."

"We're talking in circles here. She's fine. She's finally successful after a long haul. Don't worry so much."

"I want you to talk to her."

"Fine. I'll invite her to come for Gina's birthday party. She wants a little red wagon, by the way." I turned into the post office parking lot.

Mom nodded, done deal. "Maybe we should have a big party for Stacy this year. She'll be thirty, you know. My baby, thirty. Lordy, that makes me feel old."

I knew how she felt. But she was a grandma, it was appropriate. She'd been old for a while. Now it was my turn. I pulled up to the mailbox. "Remember, you're not getting older, you're getting better."

She gave me a wry but grateful smile, and dropped her package in the box.

We proceeded to Saks. The Duke would keep Jim company: he'd never miss us. Lois went directly to the cosmetics counter, leaving me to hop over her trail of puddles. She was unable to leave any store empty-handed. This used to involve many wrenching decisions and time-consuming trips back to the store to return things. Finally, she realized that lipstick would fit the bill. Shopping was always a happy experience now. A woman can't have too many lipsticks.

"Come on, I'll buy you a lipstick."

"Mom, I don't need a lipstick. I hardly ever wear it. Thanks anyway." I leaned my dripping umbrella up against the display case. This might take a while. I'd humor her, then check out the children's department. I knew she was good for a party dress. She loved buying Gina clothes. So did I.

"Honey, that's why you need a new one. If you find a lipstick you like, maybe you'll wear it more often."

She had been pushing lipstick on me since I was thirteen. At the time, I was into blue eye shadow. I didn't even own eye shadow now, but Mom was still excited about lipstick. "Why should I wear it more often?"

"Because you look pale and dreadful."

"Thanks a lot. It would just smear on Gina's cheeks when I kiss her."

"You mean like mine does?"

"Exactly." I couldn't help but smirk.

She sighed. "It will brighten up your look."

"My look?"

"Yes. That martyred ingenue look. Maybe it's not quite 'ingenue' anymore . . ."

"Thanks a lot, Mom."

"Look, if I can handle your aging, you should be able to. I mean, if you're getting older, I'm getting ancient. I could die anytime, you know."

"Mom!" I watched her try on a lipstick right from the sample tube. "Mom, you're supposed to put it on your hand. Nobody puts it right on their mouth."

"How can I tell what it looks like on my mouth if it's on my hand?"

"At least use a Q-tip. What you're doing is unhygienic. There could be germs on that lipstick from someone else doing this."

"I thought nobody does this."

"Well, I don't know. But you shouldn't."

"My germs are stronger than the other ones. It's the next woman who should beware."

A lifelike mannequin glided toward us, her painted smile twitching. "Mom, the lady's coming."

"Don't worry, they all work on commission. She needs me. Audrey, tell me, what do you think?"

I contemplated the merits of Raspberry Soufflé versus Mandarin Dreams, and pointed to the Raspberry. Satisfied, Mom dug out her charge card. The saleswoman's long, red nails clicked against the hard plastic. Mom didn't let go. She stared at the saleswoman's wrist. A dark scruff of hair had escaped from the ivory cuff of the designer cosmetic smock. Deep modulated tones broke the stupor.

"Will there be something else, madam?"

My mother and I both looked up at the tall, graceful owner of this sophisticated voice. Impeccable makeup is essential in the world of cosmetics, but this was clearly more. An advertisement for gimlets and green olives. The Chanel pearls, the imposing posture, the elegant onyx bob, this was man's ideal woman. More specifically, the ravishing creature was this man's ideal woman. She could not be a real woman, she was a man. A wolf in sheep's clothing. A transvestite, right here in the valley.

Sure, this was L.A., but we were a forty-five-minute drive from Hollywood. This was Saks Fifth Avenue, after all. There went the neighborhood.

"No, thank you, this will be all." My mother was giddily intrigued. "Do you have any samples of that cologne, She Devil?"

I yanked my stare from the salesperson and looked in the mirror at myself. Back to real life, whatever that meant. "I'm going to look at the moisturizer."

"I read an article that said petroleum jelly is better than all the expensive ones."

"Mom, it's a little greasy. Even for nighttime."

"Oh, I forgot you share your bed. Lucky. Never mind."

At the skin-care counter, a young blonde — a coed in high heels — was chattering on the phone to her boyfriend. I leaned my umbrella against the display case and rubbed some samples on my hand while I waited for her. Finally, she hung up and gave me a little service.

"Is there something I can show you today, ma'am?"

Ma'am? I looked around. My mother, the only other customer in sight, was still at the lipstick counter. She was talking to me, all right. "Yes. I need some night cream. Is there really any difference between this facial cream and this stuff for the eyes?"

"The skin around the eyes is thinner, so this cream is formulated to be absorbed more quickly."

"How much is it?"

"Fifty-five dollars."

"This tiny little jar?"

"We do have a larger size. Twice as much for only ninety-five dollars."

"Gee, what a bargain." She didn't catch my humor. Instead, she started to put the large pot in a bag for me. I decided to try Vaseline on my teeny tiny crow's-feet. "I think I'll stick with the refill of my face cream. I don't really need that." I handed her my credit card and studied the ingredients listed on the jar for anything resembling pure gold.

The salesgirl hovered between me and the cash register, waiting for me to reconsider. "You're not getting any younger."

I stared at her in disbelief, a zombie. Was this a gentle reminder of the consequences of my penny-pinching ways or a blatant sales ploy? Or was it the honest truth? I wanted to run away and hide, but I had to wait for my credit card. My mother appeared behind me that instant and grabbed the sales receipt before I raised my hand to sign it. She tore it up and ripped my card from the girl's beautifully manicured hand. She dragged my lifeless body to the ladies' powder room. Like any other, the plush olive lounge area was twice as large as the internal chamber of toilets and sinks. We made ourselves at home. I stretched out on the divan, crying hysterically, while she paced back and forth.

"I'm going to talk to the manager about that girl's impertinence. She'll be on the street by tomorrow, I promise you."

"No, Mom, don't. It's okay. I was being cheap."

"I don't care what you were doing. She was rude." There I lay, over the hill, and still my mother was at bat for me.

"I should have bawled her out myself. I don't know why I didn't."

"You didn't because I taught you manners, that's all. But when you get to my age, honey, manners don't count a whit."

I thought about the day I took control and slapped Colleen. It seemed like a long time ago. My mother stared at me.

"How did you get so sensitive about aging in the first place? You're a beautiful woman, in your prime. Not even at your sexual prime, think what you have to look forward to there!"

"Mom!"

" 'Course, your husband is way past his, but still. I think society is to blame for all this emphasis on youth. When I was a girl, it was good to be a woman: round and soft, mature and all that. Now, the expensive clothes are made bigger so you think you're still a perfect size six when you're really size ten — a surefire marketing strategy. What self-respecting mature woman will walk away from a size six because of a big price tag? You were raised in that era — you had it all, honey, youth when youth was good. But you never had any good images of real womanhood. And women's lib, well there's another hayride. Trying to play with the boys, forgetting about who's going to take care of the children. I bought into the whole thing, honey, I'm sorry. I worked to make your father proud, fat lot of good that did me. I used to think he was an evil sociopath, but now I'm convinced he's a manic-depressive."

"Mom —"

"You've got all those options now, but it's hard to be happy. It's a classic case of insecurity. Being a mother is a big ego buster once you're out of the hospital. And it's the ultimate handing down of the torch, I know. Honey, you just got to reach out and grab your happiness. Don't accept things that aren't fair, make them fair!"

"Jim says the fair comes only once a year."

"Ha-ha. That Jim, he's quite a kidder. He's a good man, honey, but he's only a man, just the same. It's a flawed sex. By the way, do you want me to talk to him about his affair?"

"No! It's over. Don't say anything, please!"

"Oh, honey, he ought to know by now that you confide in me. I'm your mother, after all."

"No, Mom, please. It's none of your business."

"Yes, it is."

"Mom, if you mention it I won't let you see Gina for a long time."

That stopped her short. Her forehead furrowed. "How long?"

"Long."

Lois sighed. "You drive a hard bargain. In exchange I get to see her whenever I want, deal?"

Anything. "Deal."

"Now, put on some lipstick." Too exhausted to argue, I complied. "That's lovely, don't you think?" I nodded. "Hmmm? Do you like it, honey?"

"Yes, I like it, I like it. I love it, okay?" Enough already.

"You can keep it."

"That's not what I meant."

"I know, honey, but I want you to have it."

Beaten, I accepted. "Gee, thanks, Mom."

33.

The phone rang in the middle of the night. I cloaked my panic in calm and answered the phone. It was Rosie Del Monica. Bertha had threatened to quit the show and they needed Mom to settle her down so they could finish the tour. They'd just gotten new red velvet dresses, and they couldn't get a replacement fast enough to fit into the wardrobe.

Mom kissed Gina in her sleep and took a taxi to catch the next plane to Tulsa. I was sorry she left so soon. She hadn't spent much time with Gina.

34.

The rainstorm moved across the Southland while we slept. The valley morning was bright and clean, with no immediate evidence that it had ever been different.

The desert was still wet, though, so Jim's crew couldn't shoot the commercial out there. They had already finished the interiors, so the whole job was pushed back. He wouldn't get paid for today and he'd lose a day that overlapped with the next job. Fortunately there was a next job, so Jim was delighted to have the day free.

First off, he marked his territory. Gina went out the open door and followed him to the corner of the fence, where he was writing his name in the dirt. I ran out after her and slowed when I saw Jim, but I was close enough to see her point to his penis. "That not mine!"

I laughed while Jim calmly zipped it up.

"That's right, little cutie. That's Mommy's." He winked at me. "I was just kidding, it's a Daddy thing. Yours is like Mommy's." I liked the first answer better. But Gina was satisfied.

147

Jim decided to go to the mall to pick up his new glasses. They had to back-order them, he went through them so fast. I bit my tongue to keep from rubbing in why he needed new glasses in the first place. Jim swung Gina up on his shoulders and volunteered to take her along. Brave man.

I packed up some goodies and a spare diaper and buckled Gina into her car seat. Rather than transfer the seat, Jim took my car. I waved good-bye. If Gina had her way, they'd stop for a hamburger and French fries, so I was free for a while. I wandered around back.

Leaves drifted on the surface of the pool: a branch was poised on the bottom of the deep end like an arm waiting to grab me. It was disconcerting to see intruders in my space — I felt violated, as if a burglar had rummaged through my drawers. I skimmed the pool net slowly around, hurling the debris behind the fruit trees. The filter basket was jammed. I emptied it three times before the water started flowing. I slipped off my clothes and dove in to retrieve the branch. Underneath was a score of plums and apricots blotting the concrete. The purple and brown splotches looked like bruises.

A noise from inside the house caught my attention. I measured the distance between me and my clothes.

A young female voice sang, "Hello? Hellooo?" Kim burst through the open door.

She stopped short when she saw I was naked. I swam to the edge of the pool and tried to look casual.

"Oh, I'm sorry! I saw Jim's car and — I rang the doorbell but nobody answered — the door was open, so . . ."

"He's not home."

Kim started backing up. She looked guilty to me. Embarrassed. For me, I suppose. "Could you please tell him I stopped by? I'll talk to him later."

I'd bet she would. Why did she come over, anyway? How did she know he wasn't working? I knew she wasn't on this job. Something stunk and it wasn't the rotting fruit.

"Thanks, bye."

"Good-bye."

The water was cloudy with organic refuse. I pulled my hair into a ponytail and put on my blue goggles. I would need all the help I could get seeing through this water. The challenge was to determine the distance between me and the wall, for turns. Despite the bright sun, the water was spooky. Another world.

Mercurial liquid weighed me down and deceived me with reflections. The glaring light at every breath was disconcerting. My world was an odd contrast to the majestic sky. Birds rebuilt their nests in the trees and insects foraged fruit on the ground. I slogged through the water, forcing myself to finish every lap until I finally hit my stride at twenty. Twenty laps is a fair warm-up, so I told myself that nothing was wrong. Mother Nature had a tantrum, that's all.

I found a rhythm, but it wasn't perfect. Every lap was a struggle, a battle of elements, a war of conscience. Did I give up, take the easy way out, regret it always? Or did I carve my own path with powerful strokes? I fought. I battled the swift current until my limbs ached and I bled exhaustion from every pore. It is true that one can sweat underwater. Evidence is in the flushed face, the hot flesh, the desert thirst. I finished my 66 laps. I was a miler, here for the long haul. I was not a quitter.

35.

"Your girlfriend was here." I smoothed a fresh layer of moisturizer on my face.

"My what?" Jim brushed his teeth to get rid of his beef tallow breath.

"Kim." I watched his face in the mirror, but except for the slightest drop of his lips into a frown, he did not respond. He was good, very good. "I think she wanted her sunglasses." I knew what she really wanted.

"They're at the office."

"Obviously, she'd rather visit you at home. Especially if I wasn't here." He flashed me a warning look. "I mean, anyone would." I meant it as a compliment.

Gina ran in with Jim's new glasses half-cocked across her nose. "Look, Mommy!"

"Yes, those are Daddy's glasses, very nice. Let's give them back to Daddy now." I lifted them off her face.

"I don't, Mommy."

"You have those red heart-shaped ones, why don't you go get those?" Gina ran off to find them. So remarkable, all these eyeglasses, protecting us from the light of day while helping us focus on the truth. I gave Jim's glasses back to him. "She walked right in, you know. I was in the pool. Naked."

"So? You grew up in a locker room."

"Not with her."

"Let's just pretend this is any other Saturday and start over. We can pretend nothing happened."

"Pretend nothing happened? I want to talk about it. You never want to talk about anything."

"I just want peace and quiet on my days off."

"Jim, that's not fair." He opened his mouth to give me that silly line again, but I beat him to it. "Okay, okay, I know about fair. Please talk to me."

He took a deep breath and faced me, clutching my shoulders with his strong grip. He looked into my eyes. "Kim means nothing to me. You mean everything."

I considered this. He saw my wheels spinning.

Was it really okay? Should I just forgive him and be done with it? Could I? "Can't you just admit it and be properly remorseful so we can start fresh?"

"Give it up, Audrey!" He spit the words at me and stormed out of the room.

I called after him. "I'd like to give it up.

Don't you think I would?"

The rest of the day was peaceful. He acted like his feelings were hurt. Ha. My feelings were hurt. We didn't communicate on an open level, but we functioned fine via our mutual adoration society of Gina. We took her to the petting zoo after her nap and had a good time, each singularly enjoying her happiness. Every so often, when a baby goat chomped at the ice cream cone full of feed in her hand, she would squeal and we would laugh together, a picture of the happy family.

Nothing had really changed; we had just decided to live with it for a while. After all, couples who refuse to go to sleep angry don't get much sleep.

36.

"Let's go to the beach today."

"You want to go to the beach? You hate the beach!"

"I'm willing to give it another shot. Besides, Gina wants to go."

"Oh, well, okay. I'll pack a lunch."

"No, let's buy some sandwiches down there." This was turning into a real event. It would be an expensive one, too.

We sang songs all the way through Topanga. Jim's car had four-wheel drive, and he took advantage of it around the mountains. I was getting carsick. Plus, my bikini was climbing up my butt, but it would be worth it if Jim liked it. God, that sounds so sexist. I liked it, so that should have been enough. I wish it was. A month before I'd bought an adorable little hat with a profusion of dried flowers on the front rim. I'd barely worn it since Jim told me his honest opinion. I kept it, but I don't wear it when we're together. I mean, why be purposely unattractive? Finally, the road opened up toward the ocean. With the horizon as my anchor, the calm sea quieted my nerves.

"Don't you want to go to Paradise Cove?" That was the private beach, with rest rooms and a snack bar, a few miles up the road.

"I'd love to, but it's closed down from the storm."

"How do you know that?" Stupid question.

"Newspaper. There was a landslide south of the pier."

"Oh." Just another everyday emergency in sunny Southern California.

"Malibu okay with you?"

"Fine. Just a farther walk to lunch."

"You can swim out to the buoy, and I'll take Gina to get the food."

"Sounds great."

We unpacked our toys and set up camp. The weather was hot with cool gusts of wind coming off the ocean. A perfect day. I argued with Jim about the merits of sunblock while I smeared as much as I could on our little wiggle worm. He insisted on getting a base for location jobs. We walked down to the tide pool and poked our fingers in the urchins, watching them fold up like sour kisses and disappear into the sand.

Gina filled Jim's pockets with shell fragments. There used to be sand dollars on the beach — not too many years ago. I remember tripping over them as I jogged from pier to pier, a daily ritual after moving here from Buckeye country. I swore I'd go to the beach every day, if only to see the ocean. I couldn't understand why anyone would live in California if not for the Pacific. The years have mellowed me. I knew that it was there when I needed it. Still, I was sad and resentful that Gina was left with only these unclaimed bits. She loved them as if they were treasures. Oh, well.

What you don't know can't hurt you, right?

When the sun reached its height, Gina snatched my hat. "Wunch, Mommy." Jim laughed and we regrouped for the field trip. They left me contemplating the distance from the shore to the white speck way out past the break. How many laps would it take?

Suddenly, I felt uncomfortable, like I was being watched. I hadn't forgotten about the nervous proximity to Sean's place, but I had successfully disregarded it so far.

"Nice bikini. Looks great on you."

I whipped around. There he was, handsome as ever. I looked past him down the beach, but Jim was no longer in sight.

"My husband will be back soon."

"No he won't. If he went for food, it'll be a good forty-five minutes between the walk and the lunch lines."

"Well, listen, thanks for not bugging me anymore."

Sean sat down next to me. I had an impulse to stand up, anything to be on a different level than he was.

"Audrey, I don't want to bug you, I want to love you. I want to make you feel as special and lovely as you are."

What a line. "You just want me because you can't have me."

"I wanted you when I thought I could have you, too." He stabbed the sand with Gina's shovel, dug a little hole. "I saw you with your husband."

"He's not a fool."

"Maybe not. But he never touches you."

"He does when I want him to."

"So, I take it you don't want him to?"

"That's none of your business." I took the shovel away, put it with the other sand toys.

"You're still angry about his affair. What about your needs?"

"You sound like my mother."

"Your mother?"

"She's a shrink."

"This is hell for me, Audrey. Even Dante defines lust as a sin worthy of hell. I've left you alone, haven't I? Are you afraid of me?"

"No, I'm afraid of me."

"You came here, into my backyard. There must be a reason."

"Paradise Cove is closed."

"Come on up for a drink. Jim will never know. And I'll be good, I promise."

It was a promise he kept.

37.

Up on the balcony, the view was spectacular. Sean's binoculars rested on the redwood ledge. So that was how he saw me. It was a dizzying day, so gorgeous. Before I knew it, I had drunk a glass of white wine on an empty stomach. I felt like one of the tiny clouds, puffed up and floating away. I didn't even feel awkward in my bikini. This was the beach, after all, and Sean only had trunks on. He was charming and funny and oh, so flattering. Therapy, thy name is Sean. Regular doses of him might have made me a happy woman.

I'm not sure of the exact moment when I decided to give in to temptation, but it wasn't out of the question by the time I tiptoed up the stairs. My personal stairway to heaven. Maybe it was the way Sean saw right past the young girls playing volleyball or the way he touched me politely on the arm when he spoke. A mere ten minutes had passed and I felt like we were old friends. He really did remind me of a young Jim. Like we already knew each other, in another life, or maybe a dream.

Maybe a nightmare.

"May I kiss you, please, Audrey?" He had nice manners. He pressed his lips to mine, those pillow lips, and kissed me in a tender, nonthreatening way. I had forgotten about those pillow lips.

"I want you, but I won't push you. Maybe this should be good-bye."

Good-bye? My heart skipped, the prospect of losing my secret admirer was jarring. My ego screamed. As much as I needed to be rid of him, I wasn't ready. Not for that. I swallowed some wine and looked in those emerald eyes. I was embarrassed to speak, so I whispered. "Make love to me."

He waited for a moment for me to withdraw my request, but I didn't. So he kissed me, soft to melt my knees, then hard, to strengthen my will.

He led me back past the couch, away from the shouts of the volleyball match, away from the radios on the boardwalk. In his room, I could hear only the pounding of the waves, the beating of my heart. It would have been fine with me to do it right there, against the door, wicked and wild, but he fluffed up the pillows and pulled down the covers, anticipating every comfort. I was flattered . . . and grateful . . . and ready.

He kissed around my bikini, and carefully slid it off, worshiping me with every caress. He had learned to stay quiet with me. I let him whip me up into a lather and blow me away in effervescent bubbles.

It didn't feel like a fuck. Or mindless sex. My mind was tuned to a frequency of adoration, perhaps love. Different from the heart-searing love of a man and a woman committed for life. This was willful, and dangerous, fragile and fierce. I felt invincible.

Lying there, tangled in strange, yet comforting arms, we both looked at the clock. Sean looked back at me and gave me a big kiss, a happy kiss, a good-bye kiss.

"Good-bye, Audrey."

"Good-bye, Sean. Thanks for the wine." We both laughed at my unconscious display of manners. What was I really thanking him for? Was I thanking him?

I put on my bikini and walked down the outside stairs feeling naked. I ran across the sand, not the furtive gait of an escapee but the strong run of a sprinter. I felt Sean's sticky memory seep down my thigh. Thankful that our blanket was still empty, I dove into the ocean and swam hard and fast as far as I could.

38.

After swimming out my adrenaline rush, I looked up to see Jim and Gina waving me in. I swam back to them, kicking on my back, reflecting on my last private moments. Then I spun over and bodysurfed back in. I pulled up my sandy bottoms and climbed up to Gina, renewed.

I hugged her with all my might. "Wet, Mommy!" She tugged at a large towel and Jim tossed it up to me. He naturally attributed my elevated mood to endorphins.

"You looked good out there."

"Water's great."

"So's lunch. You must be starving with all that exercise."

I was.

We sorted out the food that remained from their hungry walk back, and I scarfed up every last potato chip.

"Is that a new suit?" Was he talking to me? "It looks great on you. Red is definitely your color."

"Thanks." I was wary.

Jim put his arm around me, satisfied, I guess, that it was behind us now. It certainly was. Could he smell it? Smell me? Smell Sean? Of course not. I was perfumed with seaweed and salt.

After lunch, we played with Gina in the sand. Rather, Jim did. I stretched out, relaxing under the umbrella.

At one point, Gina looked up. She must have done something that reminded her of our last visit. "Play with Sean, Mommy?"

"What, cutie?"

"Sean."

Butterflies in my belly. No, vultures.

"Who's Sean?"

I acted nonchalant. "Oh, just a friend who played with Gina last time we were here."

"I thought you always went to Paradise?"

"Not always." I smiled at Jim. Yes, there was a lot he didn't know about. About me, about my inner life and about whose friend Sean really was. It would be good to get back to our old style of open communication. Somehow, it seemed like there was hope now.

39.

Jim made love to me in the early morning. The earth moved. Literally. 6.0 on the Richter scale; the house rumbled for nearly a minute. I stuck my head up to look out the window. Water was sloshing out of the pool. We both clambered from the bed to check on Gina. She was sleeping soundly. As I scooped her up and dove under a doorframe, the temblor ceased.

We retreated down the hall, giggling nervously, intimidated by the powers beyond our control. The terra was not so firma.

Jim was defying gravity, saluting me at ninety degrees, so I bowed to his passion and jumped back in bed. It all seemed new, like he was really there. It may have been that I was finally back. I slid into home plate, safe.

Energized, I got up and went for a swim. It felt innocently sinful, like dessert first thing in the morning. A delectable day. Jim slept off our passion and promised to get up with Gina and make her breakfast. I dove in, sliding into that easy world where I am slim and beautiful, secure and in love. I hardly felt my feet pushing off, each lap zoomed up before me and trailed behind, ripples in my wake. Days like this, I thought I was born with perfect rhythm. Born to stroke. The world was my swimming pool.

40.

My hair was still wet when I joined Club Mom at the park. Sean waved to me from the ice cream truck as Gina bolted from my arms to join her friends in the sand. I smiled and waved back. It was easy. No longer was I afraid of the inevitable. The future was past; the present was as clear and vivid as the summer sky. I'm not sure if my relief was from getting even or from the flattering desire. Certainly, I felt proud and whole, the sexual being that is woman. I was wanted by Jim. I was secure. For a while there I'd thought the whole episode would never end.

"What would you do if your husband had an affair?"

"Excuse me?"

"What would you do, Milena?"

"I asked you guys. Out of all of us, odds are that somebody will."

Or did. This was not a conversation anyone was anxious to jump into. There was an obvious reluctance to consider the situation plausible. We looked around and resigned ourselves to answering Milena's challenge.

Kathy shrugged. "I wouldn't be a victim, that's for sure. I'd do something about it."

"Like what?" I tried to sound nonchalant.

"Like, blow a few thousand on clothes, take a trip to Hawaii, first-class of course."

"What happens when you run out of money?"

"That would be his problem."

"Not if you were starving."

"Oh, we wouldn't be starving, he just wouldn't be able to buy any more stereo equipment, something like that."

"I'd rather see my husband commit burglary and go to jail." Kathy was way ahead of me.

"No, you wouldn't!"

"Yes, I would! Then I would have no reason to blame myself. I mean, even if I told him to do it, he'd be stupid to listen, so it would be his fault."

"If a husband has an affair, why does it have to be the wife's fault? Can't he just be a prick with a lapse of conscience?"

"What if the wife has an affair?" Me. Daring or just stupid?

"We're talking about husbands."

"Can we change the subject?"

"Is there a reason you want to avoid this subject, Cynthia?"

"Knock it off, Milena."

"It's okay, Audrey, I can stand up for myself. Milena, it's a beautiful day, the kids are happy, let's be happy, okay? I've had enough of your probing psychobabble. Personally, I wouldn't mind if you just disappeared."

We all looked at Cynthia, surprised. Milena got up in a huff.

"Come on, Jason, let's go swing."

Milena dragged her son from his sand bucket and carried him over to the swings. "No, Mommy, no!" She deposited him in the toddler seat and pushed him. Finally, he forgot about his sand castle and smiled. We all looked at Cynthia with respect and wariness.

"That was pretty brazen."

"I'm sorry, I'm just sick of her. Day-to-day living is enough of a struggle without her stirring up trouble all the time. She's not so superior — I mean, look at her hips. She's a cow!"

We all laughed with Cynthia. It was dismaying that we could let the woman, our friend, slip into mediocrity because of her physical attributes. It was too easy. Too sexist.

"You're just mad."

"I know. I just don't feel like a debate today. Hannah kept me up all night with her teething. I want to relax."

"Fair enough. So. Anybody go to the movies lately?" Everybody laughed, but the joke was on us. Moms are the reason that video rental stores stay in business.

"I made some oatmeal cookies, want one?"

Oral pacification, handed down through the generations. I was no innocent. "Sure. Thanks."

Of course, when the kids saw the cookies we had to declare snack time. We assuaged our Mommy guilt by collecting meager promises of eating turkey sandwiches later on. A sugar rush followed, so we all ran out into the deserted softball field for a few games of Ring Around the Rosy.

Life was sweet.

41.

The two of us strolled home leisurely, with Gina pointing out every bird on every tree. I could spot them faster, but she could hear them before my ears were even tuned in. I gave her a twig and we had a sword fight. *En garde!*

Jim drove up as I finished reading "Humpty Dumpty," rocking Gina in the big chair. I glanced quickly out the window, confirming his signature engine noise, hoping she was too involved with the king's horses to notice. She was singing to herself as I laid her down in the crib. As soon as her head hit, she jumped right back up and bounced on the mattress, hanging on to the rail for leverage. I shook my head. "Nap time, baby. We'll play later."

The front door opened and Jim called out. "Babies!"

"Yeah! Daddy! Come 'ere, Daddy!"

Without an ounce of resistance, he bounded into the room and filled her outstretched arms. He lifted her high, covered her with kisses. She hugged him hard and tight.

"Give Daddy a kiss, Gina." She put her cheek

up for another smack. "No, you kiss Daddy." She put her lips to his cheek and I heard a sweet smack. Jim melted. I motioned for him to put her back down for nap time. The phone rang and I left them.

"Hello?" I answered the phone in the bedroom, still dwelling on the tender scene in the nursery. Things were going just swimmingly. Maybe it was time to confess. Then Jim could confess and we'd start out once again on even ground. That would be the honest thing to do. We used to pride ourselves on honesty. At least I did. I think Jim did.

"Hi, Audrey, is Jim there? It's Kim."

Steel reinforcements braced my belly. He would have to confess to me first. After all, he started it. His was a real affair, mine was a retributional fling. Can't say I didn't enjoy it, but it wasn't part of my life. It was . . . extra. I took a deep breath and spoke politely, yet reservedly. We hadn't heard from Kim in a good while. At least I hadn't.

I went to get Jim. He was having a bit of trouble extricating himself from Gina. She simply refused to let go of him, and I don't blame her. She knew a good thing when she hugged it. I pried her fingers from his neck and told him to get the phone. He left in the direction of the office.

"It's in the bedroom!"

"Hang it up, will you? I need to make some work calls."

Back in the nursery, I swung Gina around so that she was flying like Peter Pan, then lowered her slowly back down to her mattress.

"Nap time, little girl." She grabbed her sucker and lay down. I covered her and went to hang up the phone. I was tired and figured I might as well lie down for a few minutes while I had the time, so I did. I reached out for the phone and put my ear to the receiver to be sure he had picked it up. He had.

"Long time no talk." Jim, casual and friendly, if cautious. My fault, I guess.

"I've been sort of afraid to call you."

Good, the whore had a conscience. Mine told me to hang up. I ignored it.

"You were really nice to me and I really appreciate it," Kim's voice chirped. "I feel really bad that — that I came on to you like that. I thought maybe you were nice to me because you wanted me. I really feel like an idiot, and I want to apologize."

I pulled the receiver from my ear and stared at it. What? I listened again to be sure.

"I really hope you won't hold it against me. I'd still like to be friends, and — I need you as a reference."

My husband laughed, an engaging, understanding chuckle. "Kim, I was flattered. Chalk it up to experience, all right? No harm done."

No harm done. No harm done. No harm done. I heard those words over and over until finally the meaning exploded and they were just alien sounds strung together in ugly meter. I hung up the phone and broke into a sweat. My stomach was queasy. I ran to the bathroom and threw up oatmeal cookies and a turkey sandwich.

Jim came to look for me, leaned in the doorway. "You all right?"

I nodded, my eyes tearing as I wiped my mouth. "Must have eaten something funny."

Concerned, he came in, felt my forehead for a fever. "Feel better now?"

I nodded, still unable to speak. He helped me up. I leaned over and brushed my teeth. "Maybe you should take it easy for a while."

I nodded, and spit out the toothpaste. I looked in the mirror. My reflection was flushed. Was that me? The guilty one?

"I heard you hang up. Gina took a while to calm down, huh?" I nodded. Thanks for the escape. "Did you hear any of the conversation?"

"I'm not sure," I squeaked.

He took my ill ease for a reaction to my nervous stomach. He stroked my hair, soothing and kind. He took my hand and led me to the bedroom, helped me take off my shoes and lay down.

"Remember when you said Kim was after me?"

I shrugged.

"Well, anyway, you were right. When you

asked me if I was having an affair, I didn't know what to say except no. I mean, you were so perceptive about the situation. You warned me, and I didn't listen. I was too embarrassed to admit she was here when you were gone. I knew it would look bad, and you seemed so . . . fragile all of a sudden. I didn't know how to get out of the lie — the only time I lied before was about your gray hair."

"Great."

"Anyway, that's why I got so mad that night. I'm sorry about running off to the hotel."

He hugged me, and I let him. I was limp, how could I stop him?

"Kim apologized. I guess she's used to men wanting to get in her pants. I'm sure you had the same problem when you were — single."

At least he didn't say when I was young.

"It's hard to be friends with someone of the opposite sex without sex rearing its ugly head at some point."

True, true.

"Anyway, I'm glad you didn't press it, and I'm sorry I let it come between us. I know you're not petty and that you trust me. I just couldn't admit that you were right. Call it pride. I love you with all my heart, Audrey."

He held me close and kissed me. My eyes started leaking, salty drips he mistook for happiness. My nose stuffed up from sobbing. He kissed me long on the mouth. I saw myself breaststroking across the pool deep under the water, holding my breath. A stream of air escaping from my lips marked my path on the surface above. I turned around and darted back the other way, submerged and struggling from the formidable weight of my wedding ring. I nearly drowned in my own tears.

I had won and lost all in the same moment. Like when I was fourteen, at the top of my form at a sun-swept meet in the green hills of Wooster. I won the 100-meter breaststroke against tall, muscular girls trying to psych me out with stretches and overwhelm me with Ben-Gay. In the race of my life, I won the Open 200 against older girls and came back to the team tent with the two most gorgeous marble-and-chrome trophies I had ever seen. I was on top of the world. Until the blond, blue-eyed All-American who'd dropped me the week before pulled seven trophies out of his bag and laughed at my trivial joy. My finest moment was destroyed. I swore I'd be stronger next time, be responsible for my happiness. Now here I was, my next big win, responsible for my grief.

Finally Jim released me. I gasped for air and groped for the Kleenex box. He intercepted, handed me a tissue. I blew my nose ferociously. So romantic. He drew the covers up for me, but I shook my head.

I smiled weakly. "I think I'd rather go for a swim."

He grinned, relieved that his miracle words had cured me.

42.

The water was clear and cold. A web of light danced in the pool, giggling as the wind tickled its liquid trap. In my haste, I had forgotten my goggles. Chlorine stung my eyes. The sweet metallic taste stuck in my mouth. I scraped my teeth down the length of my tongue, but the essence remained. I stretched out, floating, to get my bearings. The sun peered at me like a voyeur through the leaves of our giant sycamore. The net clamped down on my arms. I tried to shake loose, escape the accusation, but my arms fused to my sides, useless. Like a petrified log, I slowly sank.

Sean floated above me in Dante's Inferno. At first he beckoned me, smiling from a smooth sail navigating the second circle of lust. I dove below to escape him, landing in the wrathful circle of Styx. He swam down to me, grabbed my hand, and together we plunged down through the Abyss to rest with the seducers and hypocrites. I pushed him away and sank even lower all by myself, to the icy chasm of traitors, a whisper away from evil incarnate.

Did Jim's confession define me, or had I already defined myself? Perhaps I was destined to hell when I first doubted him.

Faith has nothing to do with religion.

43.

Shivering and numb, I climbed out and wrapped myself in Gina's Little Mermaid towel. She would be waking up soon. Jim's feet extended past the open French doors, propped up comfortably for reading on his beloved black leather chair. I tiptoed, unnoticed, to the shower, leaving a trail of frosty footprints. It took all the strength I had left to wrench on the hot water. The scorching flow pelted me until my skin turned crimson. Still, I couldn't lose the chill. Steam filled the room and escaped under the door into the hallway. Jim came in to see if I was all right. I didn't hear him knock, but I let him turn off the torrent that was just turning cold. He wrapped me in his terry-cloth robe and went back to his book. I held on to the counter, staring in the mirror. I didn't like what I saw.

I opened the cupboard. Identical gray-and-white labels proudly adorned two rows of tubes and jars. The sight of my full line of beauty products used to inspire me. I was a believer. What's more important than your face, after all? Makeup was camouflage — I was battling at the very source. Cleansers, toners, minerals, aging combatants, wrinkle creams, moisturizers, special blends for the neck, the eyes, the face — I had it all now. Still, pigment was abdicating my royal crown, gravity was sucking on my arms and poor judgment was clouding my vision. I lined up my menagerie by size, then reassembled it by purpose and finally organized it by order of use. I used to be so proud of these, now I was embarrassed, humiliated, ashamed.

I spent an hour absorbed in my task, like at five after I was to get spanked for peeing in the neighbor's bushes. Unsure of my crime, I spent hours tracing the umbrellas on the bathroom wallpaper with my finger. I never was spanked, but the anticipation haunted me for days. Maybe that's when I started biting my nails. I bit them for the next twenty years, until the day I married Jim. Jim made me happy. I was secure. I could relax. This time, the crime was certain. How long would I wait for punishment?

Finally, Gina woke up. She sang like an angel. Jim cocked an eyebrow at me as he dashed past to retrieve her from the crib. She could climb out herself, no problem, but he was always afraid she'd fall. I slunk to the bedroom, dropped the robe and slid under the covers. He brought smiley-face back for some tickle bed. I tried to participate, but my heart wasn't in it. Gina could tell. She lay down next to me. Pod peas.

"Are you all right?" The good husband at it again.

"I don't feel so good." I was suddenly exhausted. I felt too weary to sleep. I just didn't want to move.

"You want to lie down for a while?"

An astute inquiry, since I was already flat on my back. I nodded meekly. "Will you entertain Gina?"

"Love to. Should I give her some milk?"

I nodded. He picked her up and closed the door behind them.

I dialed my mother's answering service. They said she'd just picked up messages, but I could leave one for tomorrow. No thanks. She had left me her itinerary, but it was in the desk in the other room. I couldn't face Jim right now to get it — he would know something was up. I mean, it wasn't her birthday or anything and she generally did the calling. And I couldn't move. So I stared at our cottage cheese ceiling while waves of nausea passed over me . . . and through me and around me. Oh, the manifestations of guilt. We should really get rid of that asbestos-prone garbage. Another thing to add to the list. After a while, I heard footsteps approaching. I watched Jim and Gina enter without really seeing them. Gina was flushed and excited. They had brought me a surprise. They must have left the house and come back. How long had they been gone?

"Surprise!" A fashion magazine. They each gave poor sick Mommy a kiss on the cheek and left me to my own maniacal devices once again. It was a sweet gesture, and certainly undeserved.

I flipped absently through the pages, relieved by the distraction. I folded back the corner of a page with a cobalt blue suit I had no earthly use for. If I later decided I had to own it, I could rip out the page and stick it up on the refrigerator. Eventually, I would eyeball it so often that it would feel like I already had it. Then I'd be sick of it and wouldn't waste the money. If I was really mad for a dress I would rationalize the need that instant and run right out, search all over town and buy it. I'd convince myself I deserved it, and Jim would naturally agree. I traded most magazines and catalogs with the other moms. I saved Tiffany's. I read it over and over, like the Sears wish book when I was a kid. This particular suit was a little darker than the creamy Tiffany blue, but the sophistication was similar. Class is class, after all. Tiffany made an elegant sapphire set that would really do it justice. I sighed and turned the page.

A shudder ripped through my synapses, burning the trail of nerves from my eyes to my brain and down to my fingertips. It was Colleen, smiling in that serene and superior way models do. I dropped the magazine with a thud and hid under the covers until I dozed off.

44.

I woke up to the sun in my face. It was a happy sun, lacking in guile or duplicity. I took this as a good omen. I felt a bit shaky, but it was time to face the world. I pulled on some clothes and found Jim pushing Gina outside on the swing.

"Mommy's here!"

"Feel better?"

"Yes, thanks." Did that sound normal? It seemed so formal to me. Did he notice anything — could he see it in my face? He didn't see anything before, I reminded myself, how could he now? If I could only convince myself that things were normal. God, normal used to sound so boring and awful, now I'd give anything for —

"Push me, Mommy!"

Shift into auto-mommy. "What's the magic word?" I can do this.

"Peeease!"

"Okay." Jim stepped back to let me follow through. He grinned. "You're such a good mother." He stepped forward to kiss me. "Such beautiful eyes, my beautiful wife."

181

How could he see past the truth in my eyes? I absorbed the kiss, then swung my gaze away as quickly as possible with the cover motive of safekeeping Gina. "You're the beautiful one." I sighed. The good one, too. "So handsome. If you weren't so sweet, I'd think I married you for your looks." His looks were what had caused me such great jealousy. They never had before. No, I'm mistaken — it was *my* looks that led me to jealousy. I flashed him a bright little smile to blind him to my big dark thoughts.

"We're shooting in town tomorrow. At Sepulveda Dam."

"Another car shoot?"

" 'Tis the season. Why don't you bring Gina over for lunch? We break at noon."

"I don't know, I don't want to get in the way."

"Don't be silly. I want to show you off. I've been working with this director for a while now, I want him to meet you."

"The tea bag?" It was a running joke, though not a funny one, that Hollywood would let anyone with an accent direct. Not that they weren't qualified. Some of them were. British production companies earned a big slice of the celluloid pie. But they were sorely lacking in one rudimentary American virtue: loyalty. They'd ask for caviar, pay for meat loaf, chew you up and spit you out like a food processor. Then again, loyalty was a scarce commodity even in our house.

"You've talked to Annette on the phone a lot."

"The producer."

"Right. She was a coordinator when you were. You could do her job."

"No thanks." Days gone by. I don't care anymore about the dirt marks on the hero car's bumper. Stupid details. "I'll take the money, though."

"Tell you what, *I'll* take the money and bring it home to you, okay?"

Why was it men thought they did you such a major favor when they gave you their paychecks? Of course, good providers are valuable commodities, old-fashioned even, but it's not like I spent it on shoes. I used it to pay the bills: food, shelter, the usual. When stray insurance salesmen called, Jim told them I wore the pants in the family. He'd hand me the phone in glee. What, a skirt wasn't good enough?

The phone rang. Jim answered. "Hi, Paul, how are you? . . . Sure, I'd love to do a feature in town. What do you mean by low-budget? . . . That is low. Must be a good script. . . . What do you mean, no money? A little money? . . . No money! Paul, I'd love to help you out, but . . . Yeah, it's always a great opportunity. I am hungry, but — so's my family. I did two freebies last year, just can't do it. My wife would kill me. She's kind of attached to our house. Sorry, Paul. Listen, I can give you some names of some young kids — really talented kids — that might be interested. Okay, let me know if I can help. Good luck."

Jim returned to me triumphantly. "How was that?"

"That was good." I played the heavy again. "But I wish you didn't always blame me. You wanted this."

"This what?"

"This family. A safe haven. Don't blame me for curtailing your fun."

"You're enjoying motherhood."

"Of course I am. It would be a waste if I didn't. But it wasn't my immediate goal."

"You wanted to marry me."

"That's true. I love you. Madly. But don't blame me for you having to support us." I was torn between rage and empathy. He had promised to make me happy. I forged my life around his in order to receive this happiness.

But he did work hard. I wished he didn't have to work quite so hard. I wanted to believe that I worked just as hard.

Women allow men to remain children; then we curse ourselves for it. Is there a difference between growing up and growing old?

"Audrey?"

"Did you say something?"

"Please come tomorrow. Plus, there'll be an elephant on the set. Gina will love it."

"Okay, okay. What should we wear?"

45.

He vetoed the matching mother-daughter dresses Mom had sent in the mail the week before. Cute turquoise numbers with white batik sailboats. I'm sure she paid a pretty penny for them in Kentucky, because they were made in Malibu. I thought he'd love them, but I guess they weren't Hollywood cool, especially with a crew of Europeans. Who knew? I didn't want to embarrass him. Even if the dresses were incredibly cute. I took care to French-braid my hair and pull on a swingy, loose sundress. Loose clothes are comfy and sophisticated, especially around jaded crews who shoot well-built models for a living. I wondered what the producer looked like. I put Gina in a two-piece number with pink and white ruffles at the midriff. She had an awesome belly button. I went so far as to clip her hair with a little ponytail at her crown. It was a gamble that didn't make it all the way to the location, but you couldn't say I didn't try.

We drove off the main road past construction cones and around posted arrows for the production crew. We bounced over rocks coming across the old dam and down the hill to the empty basin.

In a sea of split concrete, Jim had built an oasis. Palm trees danced in the wind from a giant Ritter fan, arching over a waterfall that re-cycled through hoses to a hidden water truck. Long, lush grass lined the ground where a crane was lowering the prototype for the car of the future. There were no tire tracks in Eden. It was an awesome sight, even for a trouper such as myself. My heart swelled. Jim was looking through the camera at the director's side. His boyos recognized us from periodic stops at the house and waved to us before nestling the car carefully into the grass in front of the camera.

The A.D. called lunch. The army of hot, dusty workers, men and women, locked the camera down, turned the power off and cleared the set. They marched wearily to the tent set up by the catering truck.

Jim finished his discussion with the director and waved. "Daddy!" Gina bolted from my arms, crossing the twenty yards between them, and jumped into Jim's arms. It was great. Jim picked her up and escorted me over to the tables.

The crew checked us out as they filled their plates with tortellini and curried chicken. I felt their eyes linger on my forehead, where the scarlet letter blazed. I broke into a sweat and prayed the moisture would rub out the adulterous label. Maybe I was imagining the harsh scrutiny.

Jim proudly introduced us to some of the people, and I realized that I had been right. They were judging me. From me to Jim and back again, they measured our compatibility. They expanded their view of Jim from his solid presence at work to his real life off the clock. One by one, they smiled and sat back, settling on Gina's beaming face. Daddy's girl. She was a jeweled screen to my unworthiness.

The director was charming, as anyone making ten grand a day should be. Annette was a redheaded gal my age who immediately drew my concern about her fair skin, even under her straw hat, in this blistering heat.

"You want some lunch, darlin'?"

"No thanks, I'm not hungry."

"That's a first. By the way, Annette is getting married next month."

"Congratulations!"

"Thanks."

"I'm going to get some juice for Gina."

He left me with Annette. She showed me her engagement ring and pointed out her fiancé, the camera loader. Poised for a leap up the lucrative camera department ladder, he'd be a director of photography in five or ten years. It was not a ready-made marriage. The Ferrari in the lot must have belonged to the agency producer, not Annette or her loader. It was a love match that made me like her immediately.

"It's a beautiful ring."

"Thanks."

"I hope the honeymoon lasts forever."

She smiled. "You know, Jim was really inspirational. I was hesitant to make the commitment, but . . . Jim talks about you and the baby constantly, it's really something. He's crazy about you. I've seen him in situations, like in Pittsburgh last January . . ."

"Pittsburgh?" I remembered when he was in Pittsburgh. He was traveling out of town for a month. Gina and I stayed busy, but it was a long four weeks.

"The bartender at the hotel we stayed at really had the hots for him. And all the guys were panting for this babe. She offered Jim her room key in plain sight of everybody in the bar — and he told her thank you but he was a happily married man. He showed her your picture, finished his drink and went upstairs to sleep. It gave me hope. He's the ideal husband."

I tried to shrug this off without thinking about how less than ideal I was as a wife. "People don't really still have affairs all the time, do they? I know when I used to travel it was prevalent, but . . ."

"Nothing's changed. Even the newlyweds." She glanced surreptitiously at someone in the crew, who I couldn't identify. "And the talent, you know the stars whose marriages are touted in every magazine? Once they're on the road, it's a whole different world where rules don't apply."

"That's awful!"

"Yeah. Made me plenty gun-shy — especially with somebody in the business. But it's so hard to have a relationship with someone who doesn't understand the . . ."

"Hours."

"Right. And the stress and crazy schedule, you know. But what can I say, I fell in love. I want a marriage like yours."

"Well, thanks. You're right. I'm lucky." And stupid.

An extremely slow, smelly truck pulled into the lot. Annette looked at her watch. "There's our elephant. It was nice meeting you, Audrey."

"You, too. Congratulations again."

She smiled and rushed off to direct the driver toward a penned-in area with hay on the ground.

Jim returned with Gina, who had ice cream all over her shirt. "Want to see the elephant?"

"Sure. Did you eat?"

"You two are nourishment enough for me." He kissed me.

"You've got to eat."

He ignored my comment, took my hand and ran us over to the truck. The trainer led the huge creature down off the ramp. Gina clung to her daddy.

"Don't you want to touch it?" Jim reached out and rubbed the rough gray skin of the elephant.

I hesitated, then went for it. Coarse patches of gray hair sprouted from loose bumpy skin. Soon, this would be me. The elephant turned its head to see who was touching it and reached its trunk toward my purse.

"Looking for food, ma'am," called the trainer. "Don't let her spook you."

"Her? How can you tell the difference?"

"She's more polite. And loyal to her mate."

Did I imagine the gnarly old man saying that? Gina watched me and finally got the courage to touch the giant beast. She giggled. The A.D. yelled, "We're back!" and the troops rolled back in. Jim handed Gina over to me.

"We should go."

"Yeah. I'll be late tonight."

"I know."

"Thanks for coming out. You made my day. And everyone thinks you're great."

"No, they think *you're* great."

"Naw. I'm nothing without you." He kissed me. Gina waved bye-bye, and I retreated to the car.

The mirage on the set remained. The mirage of the good wife vanished.

46.

I was haunted by Sean's ghost. In desperation, I dug up my mother's itinerary and called every hotel listed until I found her.

"Audrey! How nice to hear from you. You shouldn't spend your money on this, I can deduct my phone bill for business. Let me call you back."

"No, Mom, it's okay. Besides, Gina's only going to sleep for so long."

"Whatever you say, dear." This attitude was a result of motherhood. Once you have a baby, people pretty much take your word for it. Even your own mother. Of course, that could have something to do with the fear of baby deprivation. "You know, I just got back from the department store, and I am so angry!"

"What happened?" I waited patiently to get the polite preliminaries out of the way so I could drop my bombshell and cry in her lap without distraction.

"When I gave the saleswoman my credit card, which says Dr. Lois Lanvin, of course, she rang up my lipstick and said, 'Thank you, Mrs.

Lanvin,' like I was the doctor's wife! I was so insulted, I really had to control my temper. Here it is the twenty-first century — I've been a doctor thirty years, of course, but here we are — and these insipid girls still think men are the professionals. I wanted to tell her that kind of ignorance is why she'll be stuck behind a cosmetics counter all her life, but I was good. I walked her through it and explained that I was the doctor and in the future it might be helpful if she considered that possibility before making any sexist assumptions. Well, I didn't say 'sexist.' I used the word 'undue,' if you must know. She thanked me and said that it had really never occurred to her before and she would certainly think about it in the future. I swear, honey, it really is defeating." She sighed.

"What color did you get?" I deflected her skillfully.

"Posy Pink. It really perks up my skin. You know, when you get older, your skin gets sallow. It would look good on you; I'll send you some. Has fifteen SPF."

"No thanks, Mom. You enjoy it."

"Oh, well. If you're sure. I will. So then. Did you get the dresses?"

"Oh, yes, we love them. They're really fun."

"Does your husband like them?"

"Yes, but he didn't want us to wear them to visit him at work."

"Why not? They're adorable!"

"I know. He thinks people without kids wouldn't appreciate them."

"Oh, well, you don't want to upset him. He works so hard. There're a lot of bums out there. Speaking of which, I just had a lovely chat with your father."

"My father?"

"Yes, says he's really in love this time, though I could swear he said that when we were fifteen. Now that he's on Number Three the world knows he was the crazy one, not me. And you kids are doing all right, so I'm feeling really good about myself."

"That's great, Mom."

"Yes. I don't even hate Number Two now. I just wish she'd send me those old pictures in the basement. My Ph.D. portrait."

"She will."

"How are things between you and Jim? Did he apologize yet?"

Right. She knew everything. And nothing at all. Big breath. "Mom, I was wrong. I don't know what to do. He didn't have an affair."

"But that's wonderful! Now you can relax. Be a good wife."

I started crying. "It's too late for that."

"Audrey? What did you do?"

"I . . . I . . ."

"Oh my God! You must have inherited those genes from your father's side."

"Mom, help. What do I do?"

There was silence on the other end of the

phone. The sound of crushing disappointment.

Finally, my mother sighed. "Oh, honey."

"I know," I whimpered.

"Do you still love him?"

"Yes!"

"What about this other —"

"No!"

"Anyone he knows?"

"No."

"Then don't do anything. Do not, I repeat, do not tell him."

"But we always say, 'Honesty is the best policy.' "

"Well, find yourself a new policy. Like devotion."

"I don't know, I feel like I should just tell him and get on with things."

"Don't be too hasty. Adultery isn't an absolute marriage breaker anymore. Many of my old clients — even Maria Del Monica, between you and me, of course — regret breaking up over one little affair when, in retrospect, their real needs were being met."

"English, please, Mom."

"Telling him might make you feel better, honey, but it will deeply hurt Jim. Things would never be the same."

"They aren't the same now."

"They are for him. Let him have that. He needs that, Audrey. You did, too. I don't know what got into you, that's a bad way to put it, but my guess is you could use some therapy yourself."

"Oh, Mom."

"Don't you 'oh, Mom' me. You know I love you no matter what, but this is a serious breach of trust —"

"Oh great, just what I need, a lecture."

"I'm sorry, honey, but this is so out of character for you. I could chalk it up to your mistaken belief of Jim's infidelity, but why were you so mistaken in the first place?"

"Um, he doesn't communicate well?"

"That's a given handicap that you are well aware of. He's a man, after all. But that's not what I mean. I could kick myself for not defending him in the first place. I just took your word for it."

Because my word was always good. Until now. I squirmed through the silence, relieved that technology hadn't thrust video telephones upon us yet.

"Something is very wrong, Audrey."

"With me?"

"Could be."

"I know. I committed — you know."

"That's not what I mean. Oh, I wish I was there."

"There's nothing you can do. It's done."

"I should have been there to stop you. Maybe it's time to settle down. Start house hunting for me, will you? Or you find a new place with a guest house."

"Mom, I'm a big girl. I fucked up on my own."

"I hope you don't use that kind of language around Gina."

"I'm going to hang up now, Mom."

"Do what you want, but remember: this is your problem. Leave your poor sweet husband out of it."

"Okay. Bye."

"Don't forget, I love you. So does Jim."

Lump in my throat. "I know."

"Kiss Gina for me."

I nodded, put the phone in its cradle, ran into the bathroom and threw up. This was getting to be a habit.

47.

The week passed quickly. I decided my mother was right. What Jim didn't know couldn't hurt him. I would see that it didn't. And there was no way he'd find out unless I told him. I would bury the sad history deep inside so far that maybe one day I would shit it out without noticing and never give the episode another thought. So I was safe. We were safe.

Bored with the park, the moms alternated homes for playtime. I had kind of a stomach virus but tried to forget about it by, among other things, playing harder. Between us, we had a pool, two swing sets, two sandboxes and a dozen ride-on toys. We also had a small-scale plastic playhouse, a kitchen, a tool shop, and a giant dollhouse. We all had miniature plastic picnic tables. We recycled paper, aluminum and glass, but we collected these plastic playthings as symbols of proud parenting. Thousands of years from now, when everything else has crumbled to dust, Martians will find this little plastic world and assume earthlings were a race of dwarfs named Fisher-Price and Little Tikes.

Saturday was Club Mom night. Periodically over the last year, we had pushed our husbands together for dinner parties and family picnics. Cynthia's husband was a swimming pool contractor, Milena's was a stockbroker and Kathy's was an unemployed actor. We assumed that, despite their diversity, they'd have the kids in common and enjoy each other's company as much as we did. They were generally polite, but after coordinating a father-child pool party while we went to brunch and a movie, we found margarita mix in the blender and realized it wasn't really working. Tonight, the dads were each on their own, child in tow, while we joined up to watch the Miss California pageant. The national pageants weren't until fall, and they were all computerized anyway, so they weren't as much fun.

We met at Cynthia's. The highlight of her house was a big-screen television. I arrived first with a bottle of sauvignon blanc, low-cal sour cream, dip mix, chips and chopped veggies — crudités if you will. I'm a mean chopper. Typically, we started with the healthy stuff until the wine hit us, then we gave up all pretensions of calorie counting and went for broke. Cynthia was ready with a bottle of cabernet, a loaf of French bread, and a garlic, sun-dried tomato and goat cheese spread. I claimed the corner of the massive couch as the doorbell rang and Kathy traipsed in. She brought chardonnay, baked Brie, and a cold minced-vegetable pizza concoction with a base of ranch dressing and sour cream on flattened out, baked crescent-roll dough. Cynthia was turning on the TV when Milena called out from the front. Kathy and I looked at Cynthia, surprised that she'd invited her.

Cynthia shrugged. "She promised to make that great artichoke relish thing plus double dark fudge. They're my favorites." We nodded, approvingly. Milena is a great cook. She also brought a bottle of champagne. All was forgiven.

We filled the coffee table with food. It all smelled good, but together it looked kind of disgusting. We grabbed our makeshift ballots as the California girls paraded out to strains of the Beach Boys. We jeered at the hokey costumes and waited to see the twelve semifinalists who would really make the show. Usually if you pick the major cities you've covered most of them. The girls from Podunk who are serious about this stuff move in with relatives or register for college in metropolitan areas to take advantage of the more bountiful funds.

"Are you sure this is the right channel?" With her mouth full of food, Kathy was ever polite.

"These girls are pigs." Milena, back in form.

"Don't worry, those two guys from Texas opened offices in Palm Springs last year. Whoever wins will get the royal treatment and be a polished professional by the time October rolls around."

"That's what the problem is. Beautiful girls out here already are professionals. They're models and actresses."

"Or wannabes."

Every girl has a secret place in her heart where she dreams of being Miss America. It's the rare girl that really wants more than the thirty seconds of being crowned with adoration and the hundred thousand dollars or so that goes with it. With all the lawsuits and public schedules of these hired ribbon cutters, it looked like only a rare, naive, desperate breed really went for it. I wanted to be a fly on the wall to hear what these girls were actually like, what they were really thinking.

"That was the sixth one who wants to be a news anchor."

"None of them said anything about the news, or reporting, or informing the public, they just want to be on TV and make a lot of money."

"With all the cutbacks, they don't make that much money anymore."

"Oh, excuse me, Audrey's sister is only pulling in a hundred grand this year."

"Tough break."

"Before this year she never broke twenty-five. Besides, she's a journalist, not just a talking head."

"What does that mean?"

"That means she has a master's degree, five

years of reporting and writes her own news."

"Don't be defensive. We know she's no bimbo."

"Why, is she a brunette?" Everybody laughed.

I nodded. "You'll meet her at Gina's party."

"So, champagne?"

"Naw, let's save it for the winner. Let's start with wine."

"We already did."

"Oh, then I'm for refills."

Everyone lunged for the food. "God, this is so great. I used to watch this and eat unbuttered popcorn, thinking it would make me look like them."

"What changed?"

"I had a baby. Now I don't care. With a little effort, anyone can look like that if she hasn't had a baby."

"Audrey, did you try the fudge? I started in on chocolate before my period and it's still bliss. How about you?"

"How about me what?"

"Were you good this time or did you eat junk food? Last month my period was right after yours, remember, so I figured you —"

"I haven't had mine yet." One by one, everyone stopped chewing and looked at me. Jesus. With all the commotion, I forgot to keep track.

"Are you pregnant?"

"I don't think so. I'm on the pill."

"I have a friend who got pregnant on the pill."

"Isn't that dangerous?"

"It's supposed to be, but her baby turned out all right. So far."

"How late are you?"

I calculated in my head. Three times. "Six days."

"You ever been that late before?"

I gulped my wine. "Once."

"Once, as in Gina?"

Miss Chula Vista wailed a show tune in the distance, beyond forgotten. I stared at my wine. Nice color.

"I have a pregnancy test." All eyes on Cynthia. "I was late two months ago and I bought the double kit — it was on sale."

Eyes back to me.

"No thanks. I'm sure I'll get it tomorrow."

"I bet you never had a stomach virus."

"Look, if my panties are clean in the morning, I'll go to the doctor. I don't feel like taking a stupid test now. Anyway, you have to do it in the morning."

"Not this kind. It works no matter what time you pee. I thought you wanted another baby."

"Well, not right now."

"Would you get an abortion?"

"What's wrong with now? By the time the baby comes, Gina'll be out of diapers and you can get it over with."

"Get what over with?"

"Kids. A few more years and you can go back to whatever."

"I like being home with Gina."

"Well, then you'll love it even more with two kids. You don't have to stop at two, either. Jim wants a baseball team, right?"

"I'm not taking this test."

"Chicken."

"That's a juvenile ploy."

"Buck-buck-buck!" They all flapped their arms like egg-laying fowl.

I grabbed the box out of Cynthia's hand and went to the bathroom.

Five minutes later, four women peered intently at the center of a plastic square. A plus sign appeared. A cheer went up. I was shocked. So I wasn't puking out of guilt. I was puking out of pregnancy. Milena opened the champagne. The cork popped out at the TV screen, where Miss Chico was dancing to *Swan Lake*.

Swans mate for life. Jim used to bring me pictures of swans all the time.

They all chugged down the wine and lifted their glasses for some bubbly.

"Not you, Audrey. It's milk from now on."

"Spoilsport."

Cynthia brought me a glass of chocolate milk. "I'll bet Jim would like a boy this time. Here's to Junior!" A toast. I clanged my cup against the wineglasses and dropped it.

"Nervous, huh? Don't worry, I'll get it." Cynthia went to get a rag. Nothing was broken.

"Your hand is shaking."

I looked down. My entire body was shaking. Milena grabbed my hand, started massaging it. Tiny heat waves surged up my arm. I remembered the last time I messed up a toast.

"You going to call him?"

"Jim?"

"No, the bogeyman."

Just the man I had in mind. "Naw, I'll wait and tell him in person."

"You're so lucky. I wish I was pregnant again."

"Boy, I'm glad I'm not."

"I'm going to start trying in the fall. . . ."

We all settled down as some mustached pretty-boy announced the five finalists. All stepped to the center and twirled in their evening gowns. Which was legal this year, padding or boob jobs? They all had healthy chests. Like nursing chests, I thought. I searched for a further distraction. This year backless dresses were pervasive. It was as if they saw one girl's naked back, so the rest grabbed their nail clippers and cut out the backs along the edges of the patterns — be they jagged or straight, elegant or ridiculous. We got involved again, dismissing one gal on account of her thin lips and another for bad hair, but each of my friends looked back at me periodically to smile and shake her head.

I tried to get back into the catty fun, but I was distracted. Finally, I stood up. "Okay, you guys, I'm out of here."

48.

Jim was asleep when I got home, pooped from another long week. Gina had kicked off her covers, as usual, and was sucking soundly. I covered her up and sat in the dark living room, gathering my courage.

We hadn't really spoken about having another child yet, but we definitely wanted one, at least one, depending on how things went. I wasn't sure exactly what those "things" were. Who knew when our lottery number would turn up? Jim wasn't getting any younger. God knows, I wasn't.

My folks were twenty when I was born. I always loved having young parents. They were the standouts in every school class, so good-looking and so intelligent. They stood out later, too, during countless scenes in front of the junior high while my father's latest mistress waited in his scarlet-and-gray Cadillac, grinning like the Cheshire cat. By then, I denied the bloodline. When kids would ask me if those were my parents out there, my mother in her bathrobe and curlers on the slushy drive, I

206

would deny it. "My mom's already at the university; she had an eight o'clock seminar. Must have been somebody else."

Overnight, the glossy black hair of that Ph.D. portrait turned gray in patches and started falling out. No one had heard of stress back then. My father blamed it on her new diet of vodka. He, of course, remained gorgeous with no understanding of guilt or memory of evil. I hoped I'd take after him in that respect.

I left Buckeye country the day after graduation, forsaking even Moose's father's Ivy League tradition and its guarantee of financial ease for freedom in the West. When the Harvard interviewer asked me what my goals were, I told him my main goal was to go to college in California. After that, there wasn't much choice. In moments of insecurity, I regretted missing that easy stamp of self-respect. I went to a good school out here, but things far away always seem so much better. Don't they?

What would my mother say? She'd be thrilled, I bet, another raison d'être. She'd say it was perfect timing. Then she'd ask me who the father was.

My head was swimming. Time for this tomorrow. I slipped into bed beside Jim and stared at the cottage-cheese ceiling, my mind a blank for the entire ten seconds it took me to fall asleep.

49.

The phone rang early. Jim mumbled in his sleep, stretched the cord across his sprawling mass and passed it over to me. I was immediately awake.

It was Milena. "Well? What'd he say?"

"Um, nothing yet." I struggled to avoid incriminating words. Jim put a pillow over his head.

"You haven't told him?"

"Busy sleeping."

"Well, call me back after."

I passed the phone back to Jim, who hung it up and rolled over. He pulled his long leg out of the covers and draped it over me. If he were an animal, he'd be a gazelle. No, a buck. A stallion? Anyway, I was trapped. A long sinewy trap. I closed my eyes. The phone rang again. The scene replayed itself with Cynthia on the line. After that Jim switched on the answering machine. It took four loud rings to catch on Kathy's call. By then we were both awake.

"What's all the fuss? It's Sunday!"

"Early risers. Moms, you know." I could hear

Gina stirring. Might as well be now. "Jim?"

"Mmmm?"

How to do this . . . do I talk about our family? About Gina? Lead him to it slowly? Deep breath. "I'm pregnant."

He just stared at me for a long minute. His eyes narrowed, judging whether he was dreaming or awake. I could tell it was the last thing he expected to hear. Then he smiled. "You sure?"

I got up out of bed to get my little plastic proof. I was conscious of my nakedness, my flat belly and small breasts belying the truth. I handed it to him. He recognized the device from several years ago, when he'd proudly carried Gina's announcement in his shirt pocket right up until the day she was born. He kissed it and grabbed me, stopping himself before crushing me with an ardent hug, careful of my tender state, his holy vessel.

"This is wonderful! How do you feel? Are you all right? Let me fix you some breakfast."

"I'm really not hungry. Actually, I think I've lost a few pounds from being nauseous."

"Hell of a virus. A baby virus. I thought you were on the —"

"Yup. I guess I'm in the two percent that —"

"Nothing's foolproof. Or baby-proof, obviously." He blew on his knuckles and polished them on his naked chest. "Not for a stud like me."

His spirit was infectious. I nestled close to

him. "That must be it. My studly husband." Other thoughts crowded my vision, I pushed them away. "So what do you think? A boy this time?"

"I'd like a boy, so he can take care of you when I'm gone."

"That's sweet, but you're going to live to be a crotchety old man."

"You probably want another girl because we've got all the clothes, right?"

"It would be cheaper. Besides, I'm not sure I'd know what to do with a boy. I didn't know if boys held their thing to pee or not until I saw you."

"You'll catch on."

"What do you really want?"

"Healthy. Healthy is all I ask."

I thanked God for what he didn't ask.

"Shall we tell Gina?"

"I don't know. It's kind of early."

"How early is it?"

"I don't know." Another detail to work out. A vital one.

"Oh, you're a wealth of information. Let's call your mother!"

"My mother? I don't know where she is." For some reason, I didn't want to talk to my mother. Again. So soon.

"I saw her itinerary on your desk. I'll get it."

"Daddy!" The peanut gallery was up and active.

I rose to get her.

Jim stopped me. "You stay. I'll bring her in."

I'd get special treatment now, that was for sure. Jim loved me pregnant. The just-fucked look. Proof of his virility.

A few minutes later, Jim returned with Gina and Lois's itinerary. Gina leapt out of his arms onto the bed to hide under the covers. I found her and gave her a good tickling. She squealed and started stripping off her clothes. The itinerary fluttered from his grasp down into my lap. I handed it back to him.

"You call her. I just spoke with her the other day. She said she missed talking to you. In fact, I'm going to take a swim." I kissed Gina and got up.

"Wait. Should you be doing that?"

"Absolutely."

"Well, be careful. Don't overexert yourself."

"Yes, Doctor."

"Are you going to see your doctor?"

"Yes, darlin', but it's Sunday, I can't —"

"Okay, okay, okay. You want to call your sister?"

"I'll just send her my tampons. She'll know. Maybe she could use my extra birth control pills."

"Why? They don't work."

"I thought that was because of you."

"Let's announce it at Gina's party! We'll make it bigger, not just the mommies and kids. I'll invite your mom."

"She'll be in Alaska."

"Oh. Well, how about my buddies from work? And the neighbors."

"I don't know."

"What's wrong?"

"Nothing, it's just — isn't it bad luck to go public so early?"

"You were fine last time, you'll be fine this time. A birthday/baby barbecue. What do you think?"

"I think it's up to Gina."

"You won't mind sharing your party, will you, Gina?"

"Do I still get presents?"

"Probably more."

Gina smiled. I kissed her and grabbed a towel. "Say hi to Nana on the telephone, okay?" I saluted to Jim as he dialed.

"Be careful."

"Yes, Mommy, caweful."

I slipped into the water slowly, wary of the morning chill. No more sudden jumping or diving in. I stretched my arms out, conscious of every move. I pulled up my goggles and lay on my side, kicking the length of the pool. Things were so conspicuous through these clear goggles. Drowned bugs clung to fallen pine needles. My diamond sparkled blindingly through the antiseptic chemicals, and slipped around to my palm. My wedding band seemed loose too, jangling against the engagement ring with a series of clicks underwater. I rolled over and swam, quickly stroking up to speed. I remembered how funny it felt to flip-turn when Gina was inside me. I had to flip twice to get all the way around. Eventually, I just grabbed the gutter and swung around sideways. Soon, I would lose my center of gravity again, but now there was no problem.

I felt swift and streamlined, a locomotive barreling through the water. My nails tingled with trapped liquid as my hands dug mercilessly deeper. I showed off to the chattering chipmunks, alternating my breathing for a few laps, just because I could. Then I settled into my comfortable left side habit. I fell right into the perfect rhythm, my shoulders pumping up and down like fine-tuned pistons in cruise control. It should always be so easy. The question now was should I go the entire 66 laps. The answer was obvious: I should while I could. This was the perfect rhythm for contemplation. My mind quickly disassociated from my body. I had work to do.

If I was six, no seven days late, then I'd have been ripe for conception about three weeks ago. Give or take a week. Sean was right in there. But wasn't he wearing a condom? I could have sworn — I could have sworn to anything. How could I forget something like that? He wouldn't have been that foolish, I don't think, certainly I wouldn't have been, with the specter of disease upon us. Then again, I wasn't in my right mind at all, was I? So, what were the ramifications here? If it were Sean's baby, would we know? I hated to think about it. He looked so much like Jim. Were there hereditary problems? Would Jim ever forgive me?

I tried to think about the odds. They were on my side. I had immediately douched with salt water, what with my ocean swim. That should have counted for something. Jim and I were more leisurely in bed, more time for those little guys to percolate. It had to be Jim's. Could I try to lose it just in case? No. I convinced myself that all was well. At least, I dismissed it from my mind.

Jim was inside now, reminiscing about Gina with my mother. I hoped he remembered to ask her when to tell Gina, or rather how. If she didn't know what was going on now, she certainly would soon. Should we tell her how lucky the baby would be to have a big sister like her, make her proud instead of jealous? I didn't want to know badly enough to go in and ask Mom right now, though.

Instead, I concentrated on the party. Gina's invitations had a luau theme, so I'd just go with it, buy more leis and decorations and a bigger cake. Also pool toys and water wings, because now there would be swimming. I could chop up a great fruit salad, maybe a pasta salad, to go along with an assortment of meats for Jim to burn on the grill. I would go to the gourmet market for fancy dips and bread. We would serve beer and wine and spritzers. I would wear my red bathing suit, maybe for the last time.

I was buoyed by the prospect of contrition, as if my excellence in the role of hostess would smooth over past or, more precisely, recent indignities. I loved parties. It had been a long time since we'd had one. With all Jim's work friends it would be tax deductible. As much as entertainment was deductible, anyway. It would be the social event of the year, for our crowd. Whoever that included. Hell, even Kim was welcome, she'd grovel at my heels. It would be fun.

Like Jim always said, everything happens at a party.

50.

The sprinklers whooshed on early Saturday morning and our little songbird warbled accompaniment. The sun was already hugely omnipotent, ascending in an empty blue sky. A perfect day for a barbecue.

I tried not to look at the clock. Regardless of the time, I'd be propelled into a rush mode. Guests were due at high noon, and I had tons to do before then. Fortunately, I'd done the major chopping last night. It always took twice as long as I planned. By 2:00 A.M. I had all the watermelon, pineapple, apples, grapes, blueberries and oranges chopped up and bagged separately, plus the rotelle was boiled and the broccoli, cauliflower, carrots and red peppers were steamed for the pasta salad. The chicken was marinating, the burgers were made and I still had a foot-long list of things to do. Even Jim had errands to fill the morning. Balloons, ice, the keg, manly kind of stuff. As long as Gina was cooperative, we'd be ready on time.

I was dizzy as I sat up, so I sat right back down. Jim got up and brought Gina back for some tickle bed. The baby was too far off for her to understand, but she was excited about birthday presents and swimming with her friends. Jim had hired one of his P.A.'s to lifeguard. With kids this young, the parents would be involved, but there would be lots more kids, all ages. The last thing we wanted was an accident.

As soon as Gina heard about the balloons, she begged Jim to take her, so finally he did, thank God. The downside was they'd never make it back in time to help with much else. Children double your pleasure and halve your time.

At 10:30 the doorbell rang. I was expecting the moms with delectable contributions in the appetizer and dessert categories, but not this early. Kim was at the door with a brightly wrapped gift.

"Hi, Audrey. I hope I'm not interrupting anything. I tried to call but I couldn't get through." I stared at her blankly. "I thought I could give you a hand decorating. I am a decorator, after all."

"Sure, come on in." Why not?

She went back to her car and returned with a platter of cupcakes and a sack full of crepe paper. I was warming up to her. The cupcakes were decorated with storks in pink and blue, and they were really cute. I sent her to the kitchen and went to the bedroom. Sure enough, the phone was off the hook. I pulled on my infamous red suit and wrapped a flowered sarong around my waist. Pregnancy was beginning to swell my breasts, so I felt particularly confident. I went back to the kitchen, but Kim was gone. I found her on the porch, laying a rainbow of crepe paper out next to the bowl of assorted suntan lotions and spare sun visors.

"I guess you heard the news."

She laughed. "Yeah. Congratulations. I just love babies."

"Me too."

"I think I'd have a dozen if I found the right man."

Did she mean my man? Down, girl, she's just being friendly. "Wait till you have one to decide."

"Is it that bad?"

"No, not at all. I can't imagine life without Gina. She's the greatest. In fact, I'm a little concerned that we may not be so lucky with the next one. Gina is sweet and good and —"

"Adorable."

"Yup, definitely adorable. You just love them with your whole being, you know, your whole life — every breath — and it takes all your time and energy. It's just such a major deal."

"Sounds like a good deal to me. Listen, I thought pastels would get boring, so I kind of had an ocean theme in mind for back here. You know, to go with the pool. If you don't like it, I —"

"No, it sounds great. Matches the luau stuff.

Go for it." She laid out piles of vivid blue and green crepe paper with yellow and orange fish that folded open to hang between the waves. Against the tiki torches, the blue umbrella tables and the Diamond Head backdrop Jim had rented, the look was perfect. Everything was perfect. "Looks like all we need is a mermaid."

"I thought you were the mermaid around here."

I laughed. "I guess I am. Gina's well on her way, though." I went back inside and started chopping condiments for the burgers. I mixed the salads, set everything out into bowls and platters, and the next thing I knew, Jim was back — along with the first few guests. He gave the balloons to Kim, tapped the keg, fired up the barbecue and punched on the stereo. Hawaiian music filled the yard. We were ready for anything.

Aside from running around like a chicken with its head cut off, I was having a great time. The mix of people was eclectic and wholesome — interesting folks with warm hearts. Gina collected a pile of presents. Some of the guys Jim's age had grown children, so I put the hose in the pool to make up for the cannonball spray. Most of the children were younger, so Cynthia, Kathy and Milena went out front to the swing set with a large group. People were wandering all over. I finally gave up the kitchen and let people fend for themselves.

Stacy arrived in a taxi from LAX when things were in full swing. People eyeballed the well-dressed stranger with the carry-on and giant stuffed elephant. Once inside, she washed off her makeup, changed her clothes, stashed the elephant and blended right in. Gina dragged Stacy back to her room to show off her new wagon, but really to get her present. They emerged happily, with Stacy pulling Gina and the elephant in the wagon. Gina was doing her imitation, getting fed Chiclets instead of peanuts. I met them and waved Jim over.

"Hi, Stacy!" Jim gave her a big hug. "How's life in the fast lane?"

"Not so fast, or I wouldn't have gotten off work. Congratulations, by the way."

"Thanks." He let her go. She rubbed my belly.

"Hope you're hungry, we've got tons of food."

"Hangiber-fenchfies," reminded Gina, through a mouthful of Chiclets.

Jim looked down at Gina and saw what she was eating. "Open up." He scooped the gum away from her.

Gina cried in protest.

"Where'd you get this?"

Stacy looked uncomfortable. "It was under her bed. She asked me to get it and I didn't know —"

"Audrey, you know I don't like Gina chewing

gum. Bobby's niece choked on some gun last year."

"Sorry."

"Sean gave me, Daddy," Gina wailed.

"Sean? Who's Sean?"

I opened my mouth, hoping an innocent answer would come out. It came out of Jim's mouth, instead.

"Oh, Gina's beach friend, right?"

I nodded. It worked for me.

"His mother should know better."

I tried to keep from smiling, picked up the wagon handle. "Why don't we take this outside where it belongs?"

We all went out front. I introduced Stacy to the moms she didn't already know, then she won them over by giving rides on the new wagon. The birthday girl sat in front every time. All was well.

"Lara's Theme" tinkled from up the street. I thought it was my imagination, forcing reality to intrude on my happiness.

"What's that?" Stacy looked around. The kids had no such questions.

"Ice cream! Ice cream!"

Jim pulled his wallet out.

I put my hand on his arm. "We have plenty of ice cream, darlin'."

"This'll be more fun."

Before I could stop him, Jim ran out to the street and flagged down the truck. Then he ran around back to gather up anybody else who was interested.

Stacy saw my face. "What's wrong?"

"Nothing. Just a little nauseous, that's all." It felt like a lie, but it was true. I prayed that it wouldn't be Sean.

Children swamped the truck. Cynthia, Kathy and Milena hovered in the yard, picking up the mess of paper plates and spilled apple juice. Stacy started for the truck. I hesitated, but the moms nodded to me, grateful for my taking over, so I had no choice. I retied my sarong and shuffled to the truck. Stacy and I did the best we could to keep the kids in some semblance of a line.

Sean slid the door open. He grinned at me. "Well, hello, Audrey. You want to run a tab?"

"Please."

Stacy couldn't help but eyeball Sean as he pulled a starched white shirt over his strong sunburned shoulders. She saw him wink at me. She cocked her head at me. "You know this guy?"

"Gina loves ice cream."

Stacy accepted this answer. "Will you introduce me?"

My turn to look at her. She was serious.

"You don't want to get involved with him. He's a student."

"Why not? I could teach him a thing or two."

I tried to laugh along with her.

When the children had emptied most of the truck, I walked Stacy over. Sean stepped down to the driveway. The brazen hussy ordered a Big Stick. Not too obvious. Sean laughed and obliged, but made it clear to me that he was just being polite.

Jim returned. "How much do I owe you?"

"That'll be twenty-three fifty, sir."

"Cut the sir crap, will you? I'm glad you came along when you did." The men shook hands. Gina raced back over to her father, covered him with ice cream and pointed at the other kids swarming her wagon. Daddy to the rescue, Jim went back and cleared them off.

"Bye, Sean!"

"Bye, Gina. Happy birthday!"

Stacy glanced back as she helped Gina climb in, but Gina did her elephant thing and made her crack up. Jim pulled the wagon back to the house.

I started up behind them, but Sean put his hand on my shoulder and stopped me. I looked at his hand. He dropped it. "How are you, Audrey? Besides ravishing."

"Fine."

"I remember that red bikini."

I couldn't help but smile. "I bet you do. . . . Listen, I'm pregnant."

"Congratulations. I guess things are pretty good for you, then?"

"Great, yeah. I just wanted to make sure that

you . . . when we, you know, that you were wearing a . . ."

"Of course I was. I'm flattered that you didn't notice."

I laughed, sort of. Talk about awkward. "Well, good-bye."

"Good-bye. This is my last week in the truck. School starts soon."

"Good luck. Have a nice life."

"Thanks. Audrey? I'll never forget you."

"I probably won't forget you either. But I'm going to try."

I turned around and saw Jim. He couldn't have been standing there long. Just long enough. "Jim!"

He looked calm. Maybe he hadn't heard anything. I tried to sound casual. "What's up?"

Jim walked past me to Sean. "So, you're Gina's little friend from the beach? I forgot your tip." He reared back and punched Sean dead in the face. Sean fell hard to the driveway, blood flowing from his nose and mouth.

I screamed. People heard me, started running down the driveway toward us. Luau music drifted in wisps from the backyard.

"No wonder you didn't want the party. This the proud father?"

Sean was starting to moan. Jim kicked him, hard, in the gut.

"No!" I knew I couldn't deny anything. I might as well be honest. "No, it's yours, Jim, I swear."

He had a strange look in his eyes, one I'd seen before. All this time, I'd thought his demons were gone. They were just waiting for me to unlock the door.

"Leave him alone, Jim, please. It was my fault." I tried to pull him away. I lowered my voice. "He was a perfect gentleman — he used protection — I would never expose you to — to — disease —"

Jim drew his hand back to hit me, then dropped it. He laughed, a sickening gargle, scarier than if he had shouted. "Thanks for thinking of me."

Our guests were approaching warily. We were alone in the crowd. The word *whore* hung in the air, or maybe just in my head.

Jim picked Sean up and threw him against the truck, shattering the window. Blood stained the bright pictures plastered on the side; every confection was cherry-flavored. Friends rushed forward to pull Jim away. It took three men to keep him still. Sean was tossed inside the truck.

"Get him out of here!" Jim growled.

The children started crying. The mothers remembered their babies and gathered them up, drawing them back into the yard, away from the commotion. The men pushed the ice cream truck down the driveway into the street.

I was at a total loss for what to do. I wanted to hide, but it was impossible with all these witnesses. Had they heard? Did they know?

Did it matter?

A flask of whiskey appeared and Jim took ownership of it. Families packed up and started leaving.

I thought maybe I could jump-start the party, let this episode be forgotten. "Don't go. Stay, there's lots of food, it's okay, really."

Jim heard me. "Fuck you. Party's over."

The moms looked at mc funny as their husbands led them away with the children. I didn't return their glances, barely remembered their names. They were looking for reassurance, denial. I had none to offer. I was no longer one of them.

Tempted to leave, to walk and keep on walking, I had to go back inside. Stacy was out back cleaning up. This was totally bizarre behavior for her, so I knew she'd heard what happened.

I found Gina crying in her room, upset that her friends were leaving, confused by all the fuss. I wrapped her in my arms and sat down on the rocking chair. We rocked for a long time until she was asleep. I was awake, but nearing unconsciousness. A blessed state.

Suddenly, Jim's car squealed out of the driveway. It sounded unnecessarily urgent to me. What was the rush?

I wondered if he would leave me, and for a moment it seemed like the only fair thing to do. But he would suffer the most. He would have to live in some apartment in town and be restricted to visiting hours with Gina. And the new baby. I felt sudden cramps in my abdomen. Oh, God, would I miscarry? Stress causes miscarriage, doesn't it? Would that be my punishment? Guilt in the face of innocence.

Then again, he could kick me out. I would shrivel up and die without my Gina. But Gina needs me. Jim knows that. He loves her too much to make me leave. And he would want his baby. Wherever he was, whatever straw-floored dive he was drowning his sorrows in, I knew these same thoughts were swimming in his head.

51.

Stacy came inside and sat down. I stood up and settled Gina down in her crib. Such a little angel. Bad Mommy.

I shut her door and came out into the living room. I sat down. I think we would have spoken in whispers even if Gina hadn't been sleeping. The house felt eerie and treacherous. Empty of the music and laughter of an hour ago.

"So?"

"So." We jumped at a bang of the porch door swinging shut. Kim entered with two large, full trash bags.

"Where should I put these?"

"The kitchen, I guess. Thanks." I didn't know what she knew, but I was grateful. If she knew, did she understand? Probably she blamed me even more. The right man for all her babies was married to the wrong woman. I suddenly felt she had stayed behind not to help but to observe. To learn. I didn't want to be her teacher.

"Bye. It was nice to meet you —"

"Stacy."

"Right. Bye now."

Finally, my sister and I were really alone. All I could think of was what our mother would say. I laughed. It was perverse and ill-mannered, but it struck me funny. Lois would suggest therapy for us all. She would dig for underlying motives then remind us of good behavioral techniques. What not to do. Like not to call people names that you can't take back. Not to rub each other's noses in past mistakes. We used to obey those rules instinctively. Now, our instincts were sour. Suddenly, I wanted desperately to know what I should do. But I didn't think she'd have a clear-cut answer about that.

"So. What happened?"

"Isn't it obvious what happened?"

"As a journalist, I'd like to know how —"

I cut her off with a glance.

"As your sister, I'd like to know why."

As an adulterer, I had no easy answer. As a wife, all I could put my finger on was . . . fear. I pointed at the door.

"That girl who just left?"

"Kim?"

"I thought Jim was . . ."

My sister would never have been able to live such a lie. Her feelings were always in plain view behind her hazel eyes. I saw her computer sifting through software, trying to comprehend.

"It was vengeance?"

"No, not exactly. More like lust. Flattery. Stupidity."

"But, Jim didn't . . ."

"No."

"I thought that was why you married him, because you were so sure that he would never, ever —"

"That was certainly one reason. A big reason. I guess I, well, obviously, I lost touch."

"How?"

I shrugged. I wish I knew. Finally, the dam broke. Tears streamed down my face. Oh my God. I knew. I remembered when it all started.

"Does Mom know?"

I nodded.

"I guess I should go."

I wanted to say, Stay, please stay, it's nothing, really. But I couldn't get any sound past the lump in my throat. I tried to smile at Stacy. I couldn't.

"Good thing I didn't unpack yet." She went to the kitchen and called a taxi.

A few hours later, it was dark and I was still sitting there, flooding the chair with remorse. Fortunately, Gina was overtired from the party and showed every sign of sleeping through the night.

Jim came home. He walked in with a heavy step, and turned on the light. He didn't realize I was sitting there until he saw me. He didn't say a word. He walked right past me and went into the bedroom.

Crying doesn't move him anymore.

52.

I needed a swim. I poised my toe for cool, re-freshing water. But the water was warm, warm muck from all the bodies. Opaque in the porch light. I pulled up my gray goggles. I didn't want to see clearly. I just wanted to move. I wanted to hide from the world, just swim my laps and let my mind go blank. But it didn't feel right. I swam a lap and stopped. I swam another lap and drifted. I forced myself to do two in a row. It was impossible.

I spent hours searching for that perfect rhythm. I knew if I just kept swimming, I'd get there eventually. I had spent my whole life be-lieving that. I had to hit that mile mark, those 66 perfect laps. Sometimes I hit it, or thought I did. But all the time, I was swimming in circles. Missed it. If I stopped now, I would drown. I had to keep swimming.

How many laps would it take?

53.

I woke to the sound of Jim marking his territory. Or unmarking mine. I hadn't slept much and didn't expect to now. My heart still throbbed with pain. I jammed the pillow over my head and tried to disappear. I could get on my knees and beg mercy. I could steal Gina away and raise her in the wild. No, that was what Jim would do. I couldn't do anything; I could barely move, black and blue on the inside. Despair is nature's morphine.

The noise grew louder now, drowning my plans of escape. It was urgent and strong, like a finger to my lips. *Shhh*, not a word . . . *shhh*, it never happened . . . *shhh*, make it stop. The noisy stream rose to a flooding river, a roaring waterfall. My ears were ringing.

I sat up. The other side of the bed was empty. Better not be the plumbing. Why did I have to deal with all the emergencies? I tore my robe off the hook and tried to match my arms with the openings. Forget it. I dropped it on the floor. Jim's white T-shirt covered my ass.

The water was outside. Was he hosing off the

232

evidence? Washing away my crime? Gina was still in her crib having sweet dreams. Too bad she would have to wake up and remember what happened. Maybe she wouldn't — we did make it through the cake and there were lots of presents to distract her. Maybe she'd never have to know. I kissed her and went to find her father. My husband.

I was afraid to see him, but I had to. I had to know what he was thinking, what he was going to do. He had to know it was unintentional, impulsive, after the fact. Manslaughter, not murder. Sin in the second degree.

Please forgive me.

The driveway was wet and slippery. I tripped over Gina's wagon and couldn't get up. Pathetic. Crepe paper remnants sprayed blue and green patterns in the flow. There was no hose, no plan, just a torrential flood. I felt trapped in the rushing stream, a chilly baptism.

Jim stood at the end of the driveway, pants soaked to the knees. The water sloshed around him, an island of anguish. I wanted to shout to him, but he would never hear me over the roar. And what would I say? I pushed myself up, wanting to wave. His T-shirt stuck to my goose bumps. It made a sucking noise as I pulled it away, then hung lank and heavy, slapping my thighs.

Early morning cars splashed through the man-made lake in the road. A balding neighbor in a jogging suit struggled to contain his Labrador, straining at the leash. A bent woman in church lace shaded her eyes to stare as she picked up her Sunday paper across the street.

Jim stepped onto the curb to survey his work. He nodded to the neighbors between sips of store-bought espresso. He nodded at me, but it didn't feel polite. Then the water ebbed and I understood.

I ran to the backyard.

The pool was empty, a barren cavity. My world had disappeared. The last puddle from the deep end gushed like blood through the long tube spewing its final drops of life. The rented pump shuddered to a stop.

I stumbled slowly down the naked steps, leaving muddy tracks behind me. It was my punishment, I knew. I'd destroyed his safe haven so he destroyed mine, my water wonderland. It looked so small. I shivered.

I stood in the shallow end and watched the walls slowly lighten in the air. The drain gurgled in the deep end. The dark bottom lured me, I had to touch it, this was real. I sat down to slide, but the cement was too rough. I crab-walked a bit, then stood and tried to step down, but it was too steep. I'd never noticed. I ran down the slope, out of control again, and put my hands up to stop from crashing into the light at the far end. As if it would hurt.

The ladder was out of reach. I circled the drain, wondering how I had gotten here, or rather why. Ironic that adultery, the very act that had shaded my youth, would now color my adulthood. And I'd made it happen. I did it. I wanted to believe in fate, accept that what happened was meant to be, be free from fault, not responsible. But that made me evil from the start. Life as a game of dominoes, every path leads to ruin. What was I thinking, thinking too much?

Gina's blue hair band was caught in the drain with some pine needles. I kneeled to pull it out. The elastic was bright against the bottom. My beautiful blue pool was actually gray. The sky was what had made it so pretty, a reflection of the life I'd squandered above.

Exhausted, I lay down. The walls rose high above me, hiding the palm from sight. The fruit trees shook their branches, pointing and taunting in turn. I scratched my arms against the floor, a beached mermaid. Dante, indeed. I had finally hit bottom, this had to be hell.

I was never so wrong.

Gina's melodious voice cut through the fog. She was out of her crib, awake. Where was Jim?

"Mommy! Mommy!"

"Here I am, baby. Wait — I'm coming." I stood up, damp and disoriented.

Her head appeared over the edge.

"Catch me, Mommy!"

54.

A scream echoes through my silent limbs. It is my scream, and it never ends. I see my angel fly through the air, too fast, too small, too late.

They say she felt no pain, my tiny mass of Gina, stained against the cold concrete.

55.

Time blurs, like swimming without goggles, crying beneath the waves. A baby came during the rainy season, but he left the hospital, I stay. The suntanned weatherman warns of drought, he doesn't count my tears. When I am empty, they try to fill me, big words and small pills. I count my heartbeats, hoping for silence. Have mercy.

I stare out my window at the manicured view. Clouds drift across the reflecting pool. The water is a test, glass that shatters above a whisper. I can't lie in a bathtub, relax in a shower, imagine a swim. My muscles have atrophied, I cannot feel them. I can't feel anything, won't. I hear my angel sing.

Colleen mocks me from the billboard across the street. She laughs and licks an ice cream cone, her ebony hair gleams. My head is a shock of gray now and I make no excuses.

Lipstick and baby pictures, well-meaning prayers. Go away. Murmurs of purgatory, promises of home. How can I?

56.

We drive past the old house en route to condoville. A For Sale sign pierces the dry lawn like a stake in the heart of a vampire. Smashed Christmas lights snake through the dirt. The place is an echo; I see tracks where coyotes circle at night. We don't know where we're going, but we know where we've been. We drive endlessly in search of a bridge to cross the river Styx.

The realtor leads us through our new courtyard, pristine and white like hope. Her high heels click click click on the deck, and I try to pay attention. Ethan stumbles along clutching my hand as Jim watches, ever vigilant. He's friendly to a fault, eager for an address. The woman points out the plastic playground and turns to admire our son. "Such an adorable baby," she croons. "You're so lucky."

We pass a laughing family at the barbecue pit. Their smoke wafts over the wide expanse of sun worshipers. I want to whisper warnings to them all: beware the evil gods, the damage of overexposure, the languor of love.

"Excuse me?" I ask. "Did you say something?" Such a struggle to hear voices outside my head. Jim's words are hushed and gentle, close to my own. Sometimes frightening.

"He's the only one who ever swims here," the realtor repeats, nodding at a man swimming crisp laps in the obscenely large and crystalline pool. A waterproof tape player is plugged in his ear. How can he hear himself think? Or maybe that's a good thing.

Ethan feels me stiffen. He reaches for Daddy, perception innate from long months of floating the waves of my grief. How he forgives my maternal apathy, I do not know. But I will ease his unborn burden. He will never replace her. He will succeed entirely apart.

Jim picks up Ethan and clears his throat.

"Do you swim?" the woman implores him. "It's wonderful exercise, you know. Not hard on the knees, like tennis."

I shake off a sandal and touch my toe to the cool water. Sunlight flickers beneath the surface. Opera would be nice, or whale songs.

"My wife . . . used to swim," Jim admits.

She smiles at my flimsy flesh, surprised.

"My wife" is what he said; I heard him say that, like a gift.

"How nice," the lady offers.

But I'm not there, I'm listening to the rhythm of our life. It bursts from our hearts and bounces off the pool, beat-beat, beat-beat. It was lost in all those laps, 65, 66, stop

239

counting! Love can't be measured in a mile; there is no finish line. I am suddenly thirsty.

"It was a long time ago," Jim remembers. "But Audrey was a champ."

I look at Ethan. He giggles.

I stretch my arms up to the heavens and dive in.